THE BLIND CORRAL

THE
BLIND
CORRAL

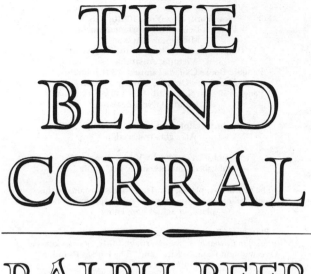

RALPH BEER

VIKING

VIKING
Viking Penguin Inc., 40 West 23rd Street,
New York, New York 10010, U.S.A.
Penguin Books Ltd, Harmondsworth,
Middlesex, England
Penguin Books Australia Ltd, Ringwood,
Victoria, Australia
Penguin Books Canada Limited, 2801 John Street,
Markham, Ontario, Canada L3R 1B4
Penguin Books (N.Z.) Ltd, 182–190 Wairau Road,
Auckland 10, New Zealand

First published in 1986 by Viking Penguin Inc.
Published simultaneously in Canada

The characters, places, incidents, and situations in this
book are imaginary and have no relation to any person,
place, or actual happening.

Portions of this book first appeared in *TriQuarterly* as
"Riders"; in *Cutbank* as "Summerfield," "Mr. Spock Calms an
Overwrought Captain Kirk" and "The Horses Running";
and in *Epoch* as "Wind."

Grateful acknowledgment is made for permission to reprint
an excerpt from "American Pie" by Don McLean. © 1972
Mayday Music (BMI) (a Division of Merit Music Corp.)
/The Benny Bird Co.

LIBRARY OF CONGRESS CATALOGING IN PUBLICATION DATA
Beer, Ralph.
The blind corral.
I. Title.
PS3552.E347B49   1986   813'.54   85-17959
ISBN 0-670-80937-3

Printed in the United States of America by
Haddon Craftsmen, Scranton, Pennsylvania
Set in Old Style No. 7
Book design by Joe Marc Freedman

For my parents and the old-timers
who encouraged me to work with land,
and those Missoula friends
who nurtured my labors with words.

I first came into these places following the men to work when I was a child. I knew the men who took their lives from such fields as these, and their lives to a considerable extent made my life what it is. In what came to me from them there was both wealth and poverty, and I have been a long time discovering which was which.

Wendell Berry, *Recollected Essays*

"Grab a root an' dig."

Henry Stamper in Ken Kesey's
Sometimes a Great Notion

I

I

When the NO SMOKING sign flickered off above Butte, I groped between my uniform blouse and T-shirt for the pack of cigarettes resting against my belly. Beyond the silver wing, foothills climbed to meet the mountains until we were flying over the actual bald ridges and spruce-blued canyons of the Continental Divide. The plane nosed back toward earth, and I began to recognize drainages winding east through the mountains. But the land made little more sense from above than it ever had from below. And it didn't matter. I wouldn't be there long enough for anything to matter. What counted lay much farther north, in the heart of British Columbia.

I lit another Camel and watched as granite peaks dropped away, surrendering quickly to limerock ridges and the muscled hills of the grasslands which flexed against the sky. I had been in the air a long time, long enough to see what distance mistakes could span. When the NO SMOKING sign came on, I decided to break starch and begin again to use the pockets in my khaki shirt.

From the tarmac I could see my father through a plate glass window, standing big and rawboned beside an airport security guard. He didn't look much changed. Nearer the window I noticed the security cop watching a red-haired girl who walked just ahead of me. I looked down at her legs; the tight little tendons behind her knees flexed against her

3

nylons with each stride. My father grinned; he had been following her too, and his hazel eyes sparked under the twisted
brim of his hard hat. His teeth made a white line beneath his
heavy black mustache. He brushed saw chips from the
sleeves of a wool shirt I recognized, put his hands in the
pockets of his Carhart logger jeans, and hiked them up. I
took off my garrison cap and dropped it in a trash can beside
the entrance door.

My father's face was serious as his hand compressed mine.
He reached over with his left and smacked me on the ear
and said, "How you feel, kid?" Until the day before, I'd been
an artillery sergeant on convalescent status at Fitzsimmons
Army Hospital in Denver. I'd lost some teeth and jawbone,
but the months of treatment had been for something else. I
was twenty-seven, thirty pounds underweight, and tired.
Even at arm's length my father smelled of horses, sawdust,
machine grease. When he turned to walk to the door, I noticed that he had grown his hair. It was tied in a short
ponytail with a piece of plastic baler twine. He walked loose
and easy. The back of the wool shirt was covered with bits
of straw and dry weeds.

Outside, the redhead was holding hands with a man in a
fawn-colored overcoat who held a briefcase in his other
hand. When he spoke to her, she raised up on her toes, and
the backs of her legs quivered.

As we walked toward a beat-looking ton-and-a-half GMC
stock truck, the sun eased into a swale on the summit of
Mount Helena. For a moment the mountain appeared to be
on fire, then the upthrust rays of light began to decline. The
truck rocked slightly. A tall, strawberry roan gelding with a
dappled rump kicked the tailgate and tried to shake off his
halter.

"I just picked him up out at Chalmers'," my father said.
The horse watched us approach with his ears laid down flat,
jerked against the halter rope again, and farted. "He will
give you something to do while you get back on your feed,"

he said and fished a can of Copenhagen from his shirt pocket. I listened to the horse breathe, watched the whites of his eyes through the slats of the Omaha stock bed until he turned his head.

"Had a saddle on him, Smoke?"

"Not for long. Chalmers says he's a four-year-old, but he's six or seven. Hellish stout. Chew?"

"I've got my own," I answered, touching my pocket.

"Could be hard to get him started, old as he is, but he'll make a good cow horse." He put in the chew using two fingers and his thumb, moved it around with his tongue until it was right, then tapped the can. "He's sure big enough. Might even be able to rope off'n him. Why don't you work on him a little? Just take him slow. He's got too much action to just buck right out anyway."

"Listen, Smoke. I'm not going to be here long enough to break a horse, let alone find a use for one."

Smoke kicked the outside dual as if he hadn't heard. I walked to the passenger side of the truck and saw his saddle cinched down to the top of the stock rack. There was fresh manure in the outside stirrup. We got in, and I put my AWOL bag between my knees on a pile of log chains and binders. The hood was smashed down flat, the window on my side spiderwebbed with broken slivers of glass. The truck lurched forward.

"Clutch is about gone," Smoke said. "Keep that rifle from banging into the shifters, will you?" I put the toe of the hard leather scabbard between my shoes and let the oiled butt of the .25–35 Winchester rest against my thigh.

"You're packing Harley's rifle?"

"Dogs. Lever-action is handier in the truck than my big rifle. Say, that girl in Canada sent you down some fancy tobacco. You know, in the round yellow cans." The gelding kicked and jumped around in the back of the truck.

"Damn fool has been fighting like that all the way." Smoke looked at me from the corner of his eye. "Hope he's got sense enough not to knock his hips down on those sideboards."

We headed north across the Prickly Pear Valley. Early September, it smelled of frost-killed hay and skunk. Rows of large, limbless cottonwood snags marked the old stream channel; a heron stood waiting in the shallow water running through the new one. I looked back at my father. Only the big, work-hardened hands on the steering wheel, the over-sized knuckles, weather checks, and cordlike veins told his age. He was well known for his ability with horses, as his father had been, for his blunt brand of honesty, and as one of the best elk hunters in the country. Everyone except my grandfather called him Smoke.

"So. How's the hunting been?" I asked, watching the country pass beyond the window.

"Fair. Killed two Royals while you were gone," he said, splitting into fourth/over with the old vacuum shift. "And a couple spikes for ranch meat. Head-shot the spikes. Earned the Royals. Got some steaks from the last one thawed for supper tonight." He looked at me and grinned. About most things he was soft-spoken, even modest. Hard work and elk were his exceptions. His grin, however, was world-class.

He checked the road and looked back, his heavy brows highlighted by a passing pickup truck. "So you're heading north to Rodeo Heaven?"

I nodded. "Just out of shape from sitting in that ward so long."

"And your mind?"

"I'm okay. Really. Things run together on me sometimes, but I'm fine."

"Well, Harley is real sick."

"You wrote that."

"Emphysema. Maybe cancer, I don't know. He lost a lot of weight this year, and he won't even talk about coming into town to see a doctor." Smoke reached up with his index finger and removed a drop that had been hanging from the end of his nose for a mile. "And he ain't going to last the way he is. It would be a good idea for you to get up to the old place as soon as you can. We've got some other problems too; we're going to need you here for a few weeks, so get busy on this gelding and get some exercise. You try riding shows in your shape, you'll get killed."

I looked out the side window. It would frost tonight, I thought, though I hadn't seen frost, except through a window, for a long time. The roan pitched around in the back of the truck. We crossed the center line and swerved back.

A yellow slice of moon showed over the Spokane Bench. With my fingers I traced out the deep, hand-carved initials *H.H.* in the rifle stock—my grandfather's initials, carved, stamped, or chiseled in everything he owned. This time of night he would be doing his supper dishes or sitting up close to the porcelain Aladdin, reading the *Montana Farmer-Stockman*. After my mother had left, it was only the four of us, evenings like that when I had been in school. We would go, I remembered, into the big log house, worked-out, hungry, and chilled. After we finished eating, my grandfather would wash the dishes in big pans on the kitchen range while Smoke and my older brother, Summerfield, figured aloud the next day's work. I would take a mug of hot chocolate into the six-sided log front room and sit beside the Windsor box stove and wait—wait for my grandfather to roll a cigarette, light the parlor lamp, and begin the real talk. While I waited, I would look at the high-backed western stock saddle hanging from one stirrup on a wooden peg fitted high in the wall, and at the photographs and trophies around it.

"All right, Smoke," I said, realizing I'd been cold since getting off the plane. "I will do that."

We passed long stacks of baled hay and bunches of Angus cattle grazing the dry fields—steers mostly, ready for fall slaughter. The moon was up when we hit the final stretch of dirt road. My teeth began to chatter.

"There's a bottle of yours in the glove box, left from when you were riding around here," Smoke said.

Behind a snakebite kit and a couple boxes of rifle shells, I found most of a pint of Jim Beam, carefully wrapped in a red, long-load warning flag. Since he'd quit drinking, Smoke made a point of having bottles within easy reach. This was probably the best-aged Beam in Montana, and I took a big swallow, careful not to chip my teeth as the truck hammered over the corduroy road. My eyes watered, and the night ahead swam in the sour wash of bourbon. *I took the first batch of whiskey I ever made to that Fourth of July rodeo at Montana City, and it sure made a hit. Half the crowd went wild on it, and I was putting it away too, until I drew that horse of Chalmers'. After that I didn't do any more drinking. Besides, your grandma was there with her folks and I had my eye on her, wanting, you know, to make an impression.*

2

I stayed close to my father's place in the valley those first few days. The stone house and outbuildings stood bunched in a grove of golden willow near the center of his half-section of alfalfa and swamp hay. The third cutting had been finished the week before I got back; piled by machine, the long stacks leaned loose and uneven. Smoke didn't care. He would truck the hay during the winter to dry ranches in eastern Montana where water and hay were dear. Horse-logging was his business, but the haystacks paid his bills.

The days passed sharp and clear. Each morning I caught the roan and fooled with him. Smoke's corral was round and solid, slightly out-sloping at the top. Beside the corral, a shelterbelt of Russian olive trees grew in an old ditch that ran a quarter mile down the section line. Off south, in line with the belt, the smelter stack in East Helena stood centered in the blue-gray distance of the Elkhorn Range beyond, like a gunsight. Magpies and Hungarian partridge lived in the shelterbelt. The magpies liked to keep company with the horse. In the afternoons, when I tired of splitting and stacking the log butts that Smoke brought in each night, I would go sit on the corral and watch the horse move. Smoke had been right: he had some action. *We had six or seven farmers helping at the chute, putting on riggins and helping the riders get on. When they got that big red bastard in the chute he kept trying to climb out, standing on his hind legs and pawing the planks. He scared off most of the volun-*

teer help; I finally had to saddle him myself. Chalmers was there watching, his leg in a cast from that time he got piled above Rocker Gulch and laid up there three days till Babe found him. Old Chalmers always did have a bad bronc or two around, you know.

Each morning I worked the horse; sacked him until he was used to being touched, caned him in a circle until he led without hesitation, talked him into taking a bit in his mouth, and got him to stand still while the crownpiece on the bridle bent his ears. I touched him and told him how things were.

Magpies would settle down and walk the top corral rail, watching the roan follow me with a saddle blanket on his back. He'd fart like a field gun throwing high-explosive rounds, and I'd tell him what a fine war-horse he was. He listened and walked, and I talked him tired.

Late in the mornings the wind would come up out of the southwest, rolling in breakers off the Divide, washing down the Ten Mile into the Helena Valley. In that rodeo wind, which raised dust and rolled paper plates in empty arenas from the Northwest Territory to New Mexico, I walked the horse and told him everything I could remember about the girl in Canada. A girl who had walked up behind me at dusk, right after I'd been eliminated from the money in saddle broncs at the Williams Lake Stampede.

I told the roan how she had stood there beside me as I unbuckled my chaps, put her hand on my arm, and said, "Hello." I'd glanced at her, kicked off my spurs and started to step out of the chaps, still too shook to deal with rodeo queens.

"Brain-damaged or just pissed?" she asked.

"Not in either category yet, honey," I told her.

"Well, boy," she said, "you don't ride real great either, but you sure do come down good."

I remembered the roar of the crowd as somebody went the distance; I remembered liking her right then, as the crowd lifted its voice and she hooked her arm through mine. I told the roan how she walked with a little limp, about her voice, which was always almost a whisper, about the finger-wide scars on her hip, and how she sent me tobacco.

And I told the big roan that when we got down to business, I was going to bust his ass.

Across the valley to the north, the Big Belt Mountains folded and unfolded. On clear mornings sunlight glinted off the windows in the fire lookout on Hogback. Farther west, the rocky, timber-splashed hills outlined a man on his back, asleep or dead. I was surprised how fast the roan gentled. Nervy and independent, he was interested and friendly too, like a saddle tramp. Each day I finished the work with a couple of sugar lumps from my prairie jacket. Every time I reached into my pocket, he'd try to bite me.

After the years at Fitzsimmons, it was sometimes hard to believe that I was out. I didn't feel much like town, but after a few mornings of horsing the roan and afternoons splitting stove wood in the woodyard, I began to look over my '50 Ford pickup. Several kinds of rodents were living in and under it, and I left them alone, although their lease was nearly up.

One evening, when Smoke got in from the woods, he followed me out to the corral and we sat on rusty beer kegs and watched the horse while I rolled enough smokes for the next day. Chevrons of geese coming off Lake Helena went by close over our heads, going to feed in Hank Simpson's wheat fields. Smoke sat on his keg and spit and talked about the gypo horse-logging show he had going up Crystal Creek in the Elkhorns.

"I told that kid who's cutting for me," Smoke said, "there's no way he could make wages with a dinky saw like the one he's got, but he's bound and determined to try. Funny though, to watch him work a tree, all the time that rig of his buzzing away like one of those windup toys from K mart."

He paused, listened to the wing sounds of a passing flight

of geese, and inspected the fringe on the tongue guard of his
loggers. Evenings, I could see how tired he was as he talked;
he spoke slowly, quietly, considering what he said. But in
the morning, the spark would be back in his eye, the edge on
his voice. "He's a good kid. One of those thirty-year-old,
part-time college students from Missoula. Wants to be a bi-
ologist or a naturalist or some morphadite thing, which is
fine, 'cause he'll sure never make 'er in the woods."

After a while he looked from the horse to the cigarette I
was rolling and asked, "What do you smoke them damned
things for anyway? Look what they did to my old man." I
licked off the paper and studied the shape of the cigarette.
"I'll let you know when I'm ready to quit," I said.

The roan coughed on the far side of the corral; my father
watched the geese and went silent. *I had a lot of trouble
sittin' that horse in the chute. He'd rare and lunge and try'n'
scrape me off. I was riding broncs here at the ranch almost
every day then because cheap, green-broke colts were in big
demand, and I knew I could ride him if I could get out the
gate on one piece.* The long-cut Dominion tobacco worked
easily off my fingers, straight and even and firm. Inside the
can I'd found a note saying she was off her crutches from the
last operation. She'd had a hip replacement finally done,
after years of attempts to cure an old barrel-racing wreck.
My immigration interview, she said, was in three weeks, on
the twelfth of October. Cigarettes that were lumpy or ta-
pered at one end I took apart and rolled again. The roan
would get curious, walk over and look through the rails, and
I'd feed him a smoke. Within a week he had the habit too.

One morning after chores, I led the roan into the loading
chute and eased my stock saddle down over the blanket. I
reached between the rails with a piece of wire and hooked
the cinch ring. He stood still as I looped the leather cinch
strap back and forth through the buckle and eased it tight.
The roan looked straight ahead, tensed like a choker cable
under strain. I fed him a cigarette, folded the stirrups down,

and smoked one myself. I backed him out of the chute and he made a few halfhearted bucks on the end of the lead rope. He farted and crow-hopped around, then lost interest in the weight of the saddle and the flap of the stirrup fenders on his sides. He stood dead still, ears back and head high, then walked to me, wanting sugar or tobacco.

Late in the second week I started tinkering with my truck; before heading north, I'd need to trade it for a faster model, a Ranchero perhaps. The oil in the crankcase was thick as asphalt. Spark-plug electrodes were green, and the ignition points had welded together. I pumped up the tires with a compressor hose off the John Deere and put the six-volt tractor battery in the truck. It started with a roar and a cloud of black smoke, the flathead V-8 cackling through nine feet of straight pipe. Mice and baby rabbits scampered into the weeds. The transmission growled in neutral and ground on every shift. I double-clutched down Smoke's lane, holding it to the floor, drifted onto the county road sideways, popped the stick down into fourth, and ran it up to seventy.

There was more traffic than I remembered on the old Great Falls highway into Helena. The orphanage at the city limits was deserted; with uplifted arms, the white stone Jesus out front blessed a dozer leveling dredge piles across the road.

Uptown, I looked at saddles at Devore's. Low-backed, full-rigged roping saddles cost eight hundred dollars and up. The shop smelled of new tack and money. I picked up a dressy red nylon halter with gold-colored side-rings, a new bit, and a fancy bridle with braided snap-on reins. My pocket was full of army back pay, and I headed up Last Chance Gulch to see how far it could take me.

Beyond a stone office building called the Power Block, the gulch looked like an artillery impact area. Holes with foundation footings and open stone basements showed where buildings had stood. Some of the holes had been filled in and were parking lots. Most of the cheap hotels and derelict bars were gone too, and though Dorothy's cathouse was still there, it now stood like an aging outcast, exposed and alone.

The barbershops and bar fronts where I had seen the sheepherders and hard-luckers, the bums and healing rodeo riders when I was a kid, had been leveled, leaving once again the gravel that had held the gold that had made the town. I stopped beside a man sitting on a bedroll. He was about Smoke's age, maybe younger; he looked stiff and cold and dry.

"What's going on here?" I asked.

"Spare some change?" he answered, looking past me down the street. "Headed back to Augusta, but I need to get something to eat first."

"What happened to the town?" He looked me in the eyes for the first time. "The buildings! Where are all the damned buildings? It looks like the place blew up."

"Well, yeah," he said, "that Model Cities bunch bought up the whole shiteree, closed all the joints and tore'm down. I'm going up to the Falls next trip in. Screw this."

He looked like he worked for a living when he wasn't on a drunk; he did for a fact smell like a real sheep man. "They're going to put a mall in here," he said and waved his knobby hand at the street.

I gave him five dollars and watched him surefoot it straight for O'Toole's to put off winter lambing and the coming of progress a little longer.

At the south end of the gulch I pegged smooth rocks at a sign where Red Drennon's oil-soaked motorcycle shop had been. SITE OF THE NEW LEWIS AND CLARK, for Christ's sake, LIBRARY. Drennon's building was gone, but the oil was still there, a stain that reminded me of hotheads and Sunday racers taking slow beers in back while they considered the innards of their 500 Matchless and AJS singles, or tried a new Greeves-Villars on the hind wheel up the sidewalk out front. Next door to Drennon's had been the only bar in Helena patronized by Hutterites on their trips to town. It was gone too, and I couldn't remember the name.

I bought two pairs of jeans at Penney's and the rawness in my guts grew. I felt the old dizziness and tingle in my face as I walked to the Stockman's Bar.

Inside, I went through what looked like a delicatessen to the bar in back. Barn-board walls had been decorated with unlikely horse collars and stained glass. Instead of the old mahogany back bar, a cooler with transparent sliding doors held chilled mugs and wineglasses.

The Stockman's had been the place where ranchers went for extra hay hands, where the Forest Service went for fire-fighters, and where the hay hands and firefighters returned to drink up their luck. But this looked like places I'd seen in Denver and Oklahoma City, where young professionals dis-cussed packaged ski weekends, their secretaries, and articles in *Playboy* over white wine. The bartender glanced at me through tinted glasses as I neared the bar; he washed his hands and asked me what I wanted.

I asked for a schooner, put my new jeans on an empty stool, and leaned against the bar with the halter lead and bridle coiled on my shoulder.

"Been out riding the range?" he said, sliding the icy mug across the Formica bar.

"Not today."

"Into leather, huh?"

I tried the beer. "Say what?"

"Forget it, *amigo*."

Some young people, Carrol College students maybe, stared at me from a booth. I felt blood climb my neck and sting my face.

"I guess I'm in the wrong place," I told the bartender as he dip-rinsed wineglasses.

"Could be you're right."

"I thought this was the Stocks when I came in."

"Never heard of it; I've been here over a year now."

The beer had no head. My face tingled, and I could feel my heart running in my chest. "Beer's dead flat," I told him.

He straightened. His glasses were two shades of pink, his

blond hair styled. "I just tap it, friend. I don't make it sing and dance."

On the street outside, when I remembered my new jeans, I felt a curious sense of defeat, or recalled, I guess, what had always been my notion of town. I hadn't been in love with the army, but at least—as when I'd been riding—I'd felt like I was out on my own. Now I was back, right where I'd been as a kid, and even that seemed diminished.

I crossed Main, drank a slow cup of coffee at the L and M Cafe, and thought about my jeans. When I went back, the bartender simply pointed to where they lay on the stool.

As I stepped onto the street again, a boy in track shoes brushed past me and raced around a corner. I took several steps before I noticed an old lady holding her chest and mouthing with blue lips, "My purse! My purse!"

3

The tack room smelled of neat's-foot oil, castile soap, and saddle blankets. I shaped the new halter and bridle to match the old ones I'd been using, still numb from my trip into Helena. Pack saddles and work harness, rifle scabbards, hames, and coiled long-reach reins hung from wooden pegs. Hackamores, pairs of stirrups, and assorted horseshoes arranged by size and design lined the wall behind the saddle stands. Leather punches, brass rivets in jars, lengths of lacing, and rolled sides of latigo leather were pigeonholed along the work bench. A bleached calendar girl a yard long sat on a hay bale, smiling at me. I'd watched through my boyhood for her shirt's bottom button to pop loose. Below the cowgirl it said: 19 DUNCAN AND SONS FEEDS 57. Mouse turds rolled on the bench as I saddle-soaped the new bridle. After my accident at Fort Sill, the girl in Canada had written once a week; she probably thought I'd be in that ward forever, but she hung right in there anyway. I looked at the calendar—at full breasts and long, tapering legs—deciding to put off calling her to explain this last delay. It was funny how we'd both been winners and ended up in hospitals for so long, how each time we tried to get together one of us got hurt. But maybe that was what had kept us going—all those letters, which seemed to have healed everything but the pain.

On the wall in front of me, next to a reloading press, hung my father's dull, iron-gray spurs. I took them down and slid

them up my left arm, found a set of bucking rolls and buckled them onto the forks of my saddle. I piled a blanket, the
new bridle and halter, and a pair of stiff, leggin-type chaps
on the saddle and took it all outside. I had looked forward to
the letters, and the tobacco too, that tasted like September
all year long. She was the only person I really cared about,
and it had taken me so long to see it.

The roan had got used to being saddled the last few days
and only half tried to kick my arm as I reached under his
belly for the cinch. I had his head tied to a juniper post and
kept him between me and the corral rails while I worked.
He watched me with his head turned back as I laced the
cinch, and tried to bite my elbow when I pulled the air out of
him. I shaped the heart knot on the top D-ring, and he finally got hold of my Levi's jacket and gave me a shake.

On the far side of the corral, I kicked off my boots. The
sole and upper on the right one had come unstitched and my
sock was black along the inside. I studied the boot for a
moment before stepping into the antique stovepipe chaps.
I'd bought the boots while on a roll with my late-season winnings in Vernon, British Columbia, when she took me
home.

The chaps were separate and laced together at the crotch,
then buckled around beltlike in back. The corral was dry
and manure soft, but it never crossed my mind not to use
those chaps. They were my brother's. Summerfield had
worn them shiny making wages at what I was getting ready
to try again for free. They were stiff with years of his sweat.
Somehow, I figured that would help.

I pulled on my boots and buckled the spurs over them. I
had trouble with my fingers. The rowels on the spurs were
dime-sized and blunt. They made no sound as I walked.
*Chalmers was drunk as I was sober by then, and when he
opened the gate he let out a war whoop. That horse landed
out in the middle of the arena and I got him right away,
classy like, with both spurs at the base of his neck. I hooked*

*him good and tried to pull his hide off. I was riding that
saddle right there. Just like sittin' in a rocker.*

*Then he come loose and started to spin. I had a hell of a
time keeping my hand off the saddle. When he straightened
out, I was still there. He'd buck high and sunfish and sometimes I didn't figure he'd ever come down. Folks were waving and I wanted to get off. Then all of a sudden he stands up
and tries to climb over the corral. Felt just like Tom Mix on
Tony with him standing like that, except'n' when he hit the
fence and backed away he pulled off the top rail.*

I lit a cigarette and pulled the felt hat down until my ears
stuck out. Through the smoke I could see the roan relaxing
on three legs, cocky, keeping company with the magpies,
ignoring me.

I walked around the circle of the corral, throwing boards
and a few big rocks over the fence. My breath was short. My
eyes fastened to things I usually wouldn't notice: the homemade iron latch on the gate, a broken floor plank in the loading chute, bricks missing from the machine-shop wall.

The roan weighed twelve hundred pounds, maybe a little
more. I led him once around the corral, twice, three times.
Then I got him against the fence where I'd saddled him,
knotted the halter rope, and dropped it over the horn. I
stretched my bandanna over his eyes, between the headstalls
on the bridle. He lifted his tail.

Some horses his size tend to be slow, even awkward. And
some aren't. As I put my hip against his left shoulder and
twisted the stirrup around, my stomach turned. What came
up was bitter, and I tried to spit it clear. The big horse took
a step. I held the stirrup and reached for the horn. He farted
and backed up. I pulled myself on, hit my right foot against
a corral rail and tried to push him away from the fence. He
settled his weight on his hindquarters and backed another
step. *I'd reach up with my hat and pound his head. I was
dead sure he'd turn over backwards on me. But I couldn't get
him away from that fence. Those rails were nailed on with*

spikes no longer than your finger, and in a couple more jumps that big red bastard had another one knocked loose. Then, over the whole mess we went. Chalmers was there, right in the way, hopping on his good leg and waving his hat. The horse damn near ran him down.

I wanted that right stirrup, but not bad enough to put my leg between him and the fence. The sky was very blue and there were geese headed north toward Lake Helena. I reached down and pulled the bandanna away.

The sky was very blue, and when I landed it fell on my chest. I tried to roll to the right toward the fence, but a hind foot landed there beside my ear. I watched the roan twist away, reins going straight in the air each time he came down. I got to my knees and threw up, hard this time. The roan stopped bucking almost as suddenly as he'd started. He looked back at me and shook his head.

Standing, I saw tiny black dots that disappeared—like watching departing projectiles when you stand behind a 105 and shoot into a clear sky.

He met me halfway across the corral after I got up the second time. He held his head high. He enjoyed me, I could tell. The third try, I didn't use the handkerchief and lost both stirrups. His head disappeared between my legs and I landed almost running. After that I lost count, but I remember lighting cigarettes and thinking about standing in the dusk at Williams Lake, drinking beer in plastic cups behind the chutes and laughing, while the rodeo went on.

He was easy to catch. I hoped he was wearing down; Smoke had been right about him, and about my strength. I'd climb on, and he'd take his head away from me, tuck it, and take off. The top half of my body would pull out of his center of gravity, and when he snapped on the way down, my hips would follow; I'd go farther out as he turned back under me, my thighs bruising against the bucking rolls, until he cracked the whip again and the curious feeling of slow motion ended as he thundered away, already behind me. *Those dry farmers were running in their best overalls, waving their straw hats, trying to haze him back. But they scattered when they saw us coming over the top. I was getting tired, but every third jump or so I'd hook him again with that old pair of spurs I got from Georges Charpentier. Out in the open he'd buck straight, then run, then start his whole show over again. In all that time I never touched the saddle with my hand or left it long with my ass.*

He was easy to catch and not mean, but once he kicked my hat while it was still in the air. I kept sliding up on him until he got lazy and bucked straight ahead, and I was able to lean back, reach up with both boots and rake him full length. He panicked at the spurs, bucked straight again, and I took him from the front of his shoulders back to his belly. Suddenly he was walking—bouncing like his legs were coil springs, but walking. Around the circle we went. My shirt was covered with horseshit and smelled of vomit. I reached up slowly to wipe my chin, and we began to work on manners.

After supper that evening my father and I went out to sit by the corral, but wind out of the southwest moved us around to shelter behind the brick machine shop.

"I told that kid," Smoke began, "to wear his woollies tomorrow. Weather's going to turn."

I climbed onto an old dump rake that had been parked for years against the shop. My kidneys ached, and I was afraid to make water, knowing there would be blood.

"I went into town this morning, Smoke."

"Yes?"

"It's changed a lot. Drennon's is gone. The Stocks is gone too."

"Town's town," Smoke answered. "Leave it for when you need it." He took out a small stone and the Case knife he'd carried since he was a boy. He began to hone slowly. "Snow, maybe, by morning. I can feel it in my legs." He was intent,

drawing the knife slowly over the stone toward himself, seeing elk on the edge of the blade.

His legs had both been broken before he was twenty. He
had, in fact, courted my mother in a cast. Although he never
spoke of her now, his badly set bones reminded him when
storms blew in.

From the direction of the Elkhorns I heard a rolling, stut-
tering series of explosions very much like the staggering impact of a badly fired battery. I glanced at Smoke and was
relieved to see that he had heard it too.

"Seismic tests," he said. "They started over by Pole Creek
this morning. I saw them on my way out tonight. They use
helicopters, carry the charges slung on cables."

"Why? For what?" I let myself settle back in the iron seat.

"Oil. They record the blasts somehow on a graph. Gives
them a picture of what's underground. So, when are you
going up to Harley's?" He cut his hazel eyes to me, sharp
above the knife.

"Soon now."

"Get to it then. Should have been up there a week ago."
Smoke and I had never been close, and he'd seldom cut me
slack. Harley, as much as anyone, had raised Summer and
me after my mother left.

"Sometimes at night, old man, all I can see for a second
when I wake up is guts and lungs and blood. I'm not sure I'll
do Harley any good by screaming him awake every other
night."

Smoke looked at me steady, the skin pulled tight on the
bones around his eyes. "You haven't done that here yet."

"It comes and goes."

"Don't let it." He folded the Case with a snap and put it
away. "I saw Dresden burning from the air," he said. "That
was no excuse for me turning into a drunk either. Now,
Harley knows you're home, and he needs somebody up there
with him."

I pulled a stem of intermediate wheat grass and went to

work on my teeth. "You ever hear from the old lady, Smoke?"

"No," he said and looked away.

I didn't say anything about riding out the roan. After a few minutes he stood, slapped me on the knee, and said, "Got to shower up, pard. Hot date tonight." He whistled a few bars of "Kentucky Woman" as he strode to the house. I rolled a cigarette, lit it, leaned forward in the hay-rake seat, and listened for the geese. They were late coming.

Mercury-vapor lights were winking on across the valley when an El Camino downshifted through Smoke's gate and roared into the yard. Conway Twitty's "It's Only Make Believe" blasted above the idling bass and uneven roll of a three-quarer-ground cam. I heard a beer can hit gravel. The driver blew a shave and haircut on the horn and changed tapes. I stepped from the shadows and a woman said, "Smoke?"

"He's inside," I said leaning down. "You his date?"

"You could say that," she said, rummaging in her purse. "Who are you?"

"His kid."

She spread a few small lumps of hash in a tinfoil-wrapped pipe, struck a match, and inhaled the smoke. When she released her breath she ran her tongue slowly over her lips. "I thought his kid was dead," she said to the windshield.

"I'm the other one. The one who's not."

She shook her black hair and looked up at me. She seemed to be about my age, maybe younger. Her hair glistened in the blue-white fog of the yard light. "Yeah?" she said and laughed.

Smoke walked across the yard and climbed into the driver's seat as the girl wriggled onto the console. "Sandy, this is Jackson."

"Right," she said, looking out at me with intense and careless eyes. "The one who's not."

Her voice carried back to me as Smoke poured it on down the lane, a laugh that seemed to hang in the night air long after the groan of the El Camino had died away.

4

There was a skin of ice on the water trough as I buckled the chaps. I put the spurs on again, and my heavy sheepskin-and-canvas herder's coat. There was a comfort in the worn clothes I found hanging where I'd left them, something more than warmth against the wind.

The horse was stove-up too, and cranky. He was sore and tired of me, but I got his attention with the spurs and kept him moving. Finally I raised the gate latch with my toe, and we headed south over the frosted stubble in the hay field. A wind came off Red Mountain, taking wisps of our ragged breath with it. It seemed too cold to snow, but that was Montana. One day sweat running in your eyes, the next you're wondering what happened to your summer's wages. We crossed a summer-fallowed wheat field at daybreak, and while I was lighting a smoke a jackrabbit jumped from behind a clod and bounced away. The roan was limbering, and when the jack took off he slammed sideways, almost out from under me. I caught the far-side bucking roll to stay with him, but lost the cigarette. The twist and pull made the cords in my neck burn.

I turned up the fleece collar and we kept on south across hay and wheat fields, through a new subdivision of row houses on the outskirts of East Helena, and up the Prickly Pear past the Kaiser cement plant and the mountain of lime-rock they'd ruined.

At Montana City, the horse balked at the overpass above

24

the Interstate. I was afraid he'd buck into the guardrails if I booted him, so I led him across. There was nothing left of Montana City except the school my father had attended for a few years. The corrals and rodeo stands were long gone. *I kept him off those dredge piles and gravel bars by the creek. Finally he just lined out. Cars and buggies were parked all around, and when we got to Clyde Burgess's Model T, he took off like Cromwell Dixon. Mrs. Schimp took that picture with her old box camera. Never touched that T at all. Went right over the windshield.*

Won the pot, which was ten silver dollars, and a side bet with Paul Christian for two more. I bought that horse on the spot for two pint cream bottles of shine and the ten-dollar pot. Rode him home that night, though we covered half the county getting here. I used to ride him clear up Warm Springs Creek to court your grandma, he was that special.

Beyond the Interstate stretched open range bordered by Bureau of Land Management grazing ground to the west and the Jackson Creek ranches to the south: rolling, unfenced miles of rocky grassland, scrub timber, and one old man. Two sections of the home ranch had never been fenced. Shared with unfenced ground from neighboring outfits, it served as a common summer range. I herded the roan on south, past Tom Flavven's place. The windows and doors were gone from the house, and somebody had stripped the board and batten from the horse barn so that the long roof leaned east on a naked frame. The Flavvens had been violent, fun-loving men who ran with a bad crowd. They had been great friends of my grandfather, who had supplied much of their whiskey until they learned to make their own. When they partied they rented whores by the week and invited the neighbors.

The empty house looked like a skull grinning across the land; the men who had lived there had all been killed or gone insane before I'd been born. I touched the roan in the ribs and headed him up a long, rocky, knife-edged ridge, a landmark called Harris Hill by old-time residents, for a dirt farmer, who, during the Depression, had turned half his homestead into a limerock quarry.

On the north slope of the ridge we followed the faint contour of a buffalo trail, gaining ground out of the wind. Bunches of red and black cattle peppered the sheltered sides of the lower hills, grazing their way down toward water.

Just off the trail, a mound of rocks marked a quarter-section corner. I stopped the roan and let him breathe. A flat stone in the center of the mound had an X and ¼ carved on it. A yard or so west of the corner stone, a new wooden survey stake stood beside an iron peg with a bright yellow plastic cap.

I turned sideways in the saddle and looked north. Beyond a squall that moved over the Belts, slowly covering the Sleeping Giant, lay Canada. Cold seeped through the herder's coat, and my thighs went numb in the hard leather chaps. The ridge, I noticed, would make a dandy place to dig in artillery.

To the south I could see most of the Jackson Creek drainage: the Ford place, where teepee poles leaned against the lower limbs of a giant cottonwood tree, which partly sheltered the trailer where Lonnie and his family lived during the winter; Harley's place, the hay fields on high bench land across from me, the buildings and meadows hidden behind the bluffs below; and farther up the creek, the timbered hills of the sprawling Schillings Ranch.

Below me, between where I sat and the granite headwalls above the creek I'd been named for, the heavy-timbered hoist frame on the tailing dump of the abandoned Veracruz mine stood bleak as any gallows.

In a stand of thick-butted bull pine I got down to open the red pole gate. On it, a weathered plank with a Lazy-H-Tri-angle brand chiseled in the center said: HECKETHORN HORNED HEREFORD RANCH.

Beyond the gate stood wooden-wheeled wagons with sagging backs, and dump rakes that rested on broken tongues. Across a hay field, nested in a clump of trees, a two-story squared-log house overlooked the meadows. The outbuildings—a log chicken house, a tall, wood-sided shop, and two small cabins—stood in a half circle around the house. Where the meadows ran together, beside a low-built log barn, the biggest horse corral in Jefferson County leaned in different directions, the top rails bowed downward with dry rot.

In the distance, the Elkhorns were lost in storm. Scattered flakes of snow began to blow past, skimming above the ground. The last four miles of rough ground had taken the steam out of the roan. When I got on, after closing the gate, he danced and shook his head but didn't offer to buck.

I wondered if Harley would see me from the kitchen window; if he did, I knew, he'd get his hat and brush crumbs off the table with it on his way to the door. When I got the horse lined out, I saw him, lean and white-haired, framed in the plank doorway. From a hundred yards off I could see he stood straight with effort. As we crossed the hay field, the roan turned sideways, shook himself, and with a rolling little buck, straightened back out. The man at the door took off his hat and held it above his head by the crown. He made a sweeping gesture with it, like you'd use to urge on your bet in a good race. I touched the roan with my spurs, and he tore up the ground.

Through my wind-blurred eyes, I saw my grandfather holding his hat. Behind him, hanging on the log parlor wall, beside a high-backed stock saddle suspended by one stirrup from a wooden peg, was a photograph. It was gray with age, but the frame and glass would be wiped clean. A horse and rider hung in midair over a new-looking Model T Ford. The horse's head was twisted around to his right and his front legs were spread and stiff. His mouth was wide open.

The rider faced the camera, and you could tell who it was.

He leaned back, holding his hat in one hand, looking off to his right, waiting for the horse to land.

And he was grinning. Grinning like from up there he could see it all: the blur of grassy ridges and timbered hills that made him what he was; his friends running and waving, trying to haze the runaway he rode; and a young woman, her hand to her mouth perhaps, her eyes for an instant meeting his before gravity took him away, and smiling, like she saw something too.

—5—

ancy this," Harley said. He took hold of the cheek strap on the bridle and the roan quivered between my legs. A war I never saw, broken promises, and a careless moment had kept me away for years. Some missing teeth and the splotch of scar tissue on my jaw, a streak of white hair and a shrapnel-riddled memory were about all I had to show. I handed my grandfather the reins, and as I swung down, I saw that he was pleased.

The roan's chest was lathered around the edges of the martingale; he held still for a change as I loosened the cinch and rolled off the saddle, then spread his legs and shook himself to raise his hair, very casual, as if he understood that he was the center of something.

"How are you, Harley?" I asked.

"I'm still here," he answered, and jutting his whiskered jaw, bony now and square as the blunt end of an anvil, at the scar on my cheek, he asked, "How about yourself?"

I dug a ragged piece of metal from my watch pocket. "Here you go. Souvenir of the Stateside war."

He inspected the iron fragment a moment, turned his gray eyes back to mine, and we shook hands under the horse's nodding nose. In the Great War he had been a breaker of horses. Like me, he'd never gone overseas, but he'd sure seen some things. He looked brittle now, but his hand was hard, his watery eyes sharp and steady. When he moved he moved with a deft quickness rare in large men. What betrayed him was the dewlap of skin above his buttoned collar, and the way his shirt bagged about his shoulders. Although the meat of him was gone, he seemed as strong and sure and careless as ever when he touched the horse. His eyes lingered on the roan's front shoulders, where the hard muscle rounded toward the chest. He ran his hand over these muscles, wiped away the froth, and rubbed the lather between his fingers. I'd seen Harley's calming influence on horses before; he claimed it was his smell. Whatever it was, the roan stood easy, like he'd been on the place all his life.

"Let's get out of this wind. Take him down to the calf pen. Put him in where he can shelter up. I'll start some coffee." He slid his hand down the horse's throat, letting it linger again on the muscled chest, feeling, I supposed, the great beating heart.

"Watch yourself he don't step on you," I said, taking the reins.

"He won't step on me," Harley answered. But as we passed, he smiled before turning toward the house.

I hung my halter and bridle on a stanchion header in the log barn. When I opened the east door for light I saw that the hay barn outside had fallen sideways into a heap of broken beams and twisted iron that looked like the nest of some terrible meat-eating bird. Sheep sorrel, rye, timothy, barley, and nettles grew wild and too green around the gray wreckage. The hay barn had stood thirty-five feet high, big enough to hold one hundred tons of loose hay. I didn't see how I could have missed it being down when I rode in.

What I had seen was that not much else had changed, perhaps because of Harley's age or illness, since I'd lived here last. The piles of warped lumber, mounds of scrap iron, scattered lengths of corrugated red tin, and hulks of rusty machinery lay in the same places, rotting and rusting in the same slow patterns of neglect. The partly fallen chicken house, that seemed would never come completely down, and the antler-littered portable homestead cabin both leaned toward an unseen magnetism off south. The milk house, the newest building on the place, erected during the brief prosperity of Prohibition, had lost most of its shingles. And resting in a rock pile, like a long-abandoned ark, was the paintless, forty-foot houseboat where my brother and I had played pirates when we were children.

Through a dusty, web-hung window I watched the roan roll in the flaky soil outside, all four legs pawing air as he turned over on his back. The squall came in harder, the snow melting as fast as it hit the dry ground. On the bow of the old wreck I could just make out the name MABEL.

In the oat barrel, half a dozen leathery mice lay tits-up on the iron bottom. I latched the lid anyway. Above me, driven into the log purlins, I noticed the steel hooks, from which with chains and wide leather bellybands Harley had supported his starving workhorses the year he'd come home from the army. That year was remembered for one season; it was still called the Winter of 1919.

Once they got down on you . . . He'd been all alone, snowed in with starving stock and dying horses and the hard-frozen graves of his parents. . . . *they stayed down.*

The roan stood and shook himself and looked about with interest at his new home. I decided to let him pick around in the weeds by the creek and fend for himself. There was no sense spoiling him with grain.

The year the United States put the Columbia space shuttle in orbit for the first time, the Montana Power Company ran the first electric line down the creek. The first thing I saw inside the house was new Romex running up the log walls and along the broad-axed ceiling beams to naked two-hundred-watt bulbs. Harley jerked a pull string on, off, on. "Now I can see what I'm doing," he explained.

I smiled to see him proud of electric lights, but he'd lived alone a long time, and a life alone in the hills makes odd things special.

"Got running water too," he announced. He turned a tap above an ancient porcelain sink and stepped back. The faucet released a blast of air followed by spastic jets of water that splashed from the shallow sink and sprayed onto the floor.

Harley twisted the tap closed and winked. "No more packing water or frozen pump handles. Should of had this years ago. Now take a look at my system."

He kicked back a throw rug, exposing the trap door. I took hold of the iron ring and lifted the door open. Cobwebs stretched and broke as the underside turned upward; a barn spider the size of a shrew waddled off onto the kitchen floor, and the flat odors of damp stone, mold, and dead air rose around us.

Harley went down three steps, pulled a string, and the cellar lit up. I followed, ducking to stay clear of webs and the flies and millers they'd caught. Against one stone wall a small pressure tank rested on half a fifty-five-gallon barrel. Black plastic pipe ran from a break in the wall to the tank. Harley pointed at this pipe. I could see he was going to explain how it worked, and he did.

Carefully, with his fingers, he traced the route the water took.

I looked around as he talked. The wooden bins of sand for storing potatoes and carrots had fallen apart, spilling the sand onto the uneven stone floor. Crocks that had once held waterglass for keeping eggs stood upside down on mildewed boards. On a shelf to one side, some dust-covered canning jars held blue and purple fruit. The fruit had been there as long as I could remember.

I looked back when Harley said the old well had gone sour. "Pump stem fell down the hole, and I said *fine*. Got on my new telephone and called Lindsey. Had him *drill* me one. Hundred feet deep, too." Beyond the crocks, the back wall had sloughed in, covering the floor with a couple feet of rotten rock. Harley had dug the original well by hand. And, like the cellar, he'd dug it through solid hardrock with a single jack, iron drills, and powder.

"What's in these bottles?" I asked, picking up one of the canning jars. I shook the stuff inside; it looked like laboratory specimens of large, malignant growths.

"Plums," Harley answered. "Nasty looking, ain't it?"

He took the jar from my hand and placed it back on the shelf where it had been. "How long you going to be around?" he asked.

"Couple weeks, maybe, at the outside. I have an immigration hearing at the border soon, should be up there now, I guess."

"Well, Pilgrim, I'm going to need a hand the next ten days or so. Got to fix up those corrals and bring in my cows." He put his big hands in his overalls pockets as if embarrassed. "We'll work on it together. I just need some help is all."

I took a cigarette from my shirt pocket and looked at my hospital-soft hands. Harley looked at the Camel, then at me. "You knew we put Summerfield down beside your grandma?"

"It wasn't right."

"Not right?" Harley leaned toward me until his finely shaped aquiline nose was six inches from my eye. "You mean the way you took off when your brother was coming home in a box? Or the way you joined up before we could get him underground?"

I stepped back. "He was my brother, Harley. Not yours." Harley's face turned the deep red of cheap wine. "And you didn't have to write all those sole-surviving-son letters either. I wanted to go." He opened his snaggy old mouth but only air came out. I saw that the anger stinging my eyes had hurt him too. "I'm sorry," I said. "Forget it."

"I won't forget it," Harley answered, and although he was in his eighties, I saw he still had me on height. It seemed right; I hadn't been back an hour and we'd had a scrap. Smoke said the way Harley and I got along was because we were too much alike, but I'd never been able to see that.

"Am I working for you or not?"

"Yes, you are working for me," my grandfather said, yet his face did not relax. My brother Summerfield had been four years older, and Harley had taken pride in him. Summer had an undershot jaw like a bull trout and the round-shouldered strength of a bull rider. We'd done a lot together, and he'd shown me many things, including the boreholes cut by Harley's twist drills, which still showed in the cellar's granite walls.

6

Upstairs, I opened the door to the room Summer and I had shared and dropped my saddle on the floor beside the east window. Harley claimed he put us on that side of the house so the sun would wake us first. And usually it did; we'd be up and out most mornings before Harley stirred. But then a lot of nights my brother and I fell asleep listening to the sounds of Harley working in the big shop.

The room appeared to have been shut a long time. A heavy layer of dust blanketed the bunks and chairs, the table where homework most often waited untouched, and the uneven shiplap floor. To one side of the room, Summer's weights and press bench stood as he had left them the spring he enlisted, still organized for the workouts he left behind.

I stripped the lower bunk, swept a shopping bag of dust and dust balls from the walls and floor, and, with one of the rotten sheets, dusted down the furniture. On Summer's half of the table, a framed color photograph of a slender, red-haired girl rested beside a new telephone. The girl, sitting on top a haystack, looked familiar, but the picture wasn't very clear. I took a folded paper from my wallet, spread it on the table, and dialed the long number. Outside, I could see the roan walking from the creek toward the barn, swishing his tail lazily in the late sun that had followed the little storm. A familiar, muted voice said hello in my ear.

"How's the gimp there, girl?"

"Braindamage? Where are you?"

The roan stopped and I saw a black cat walking toward him from the tin-sided shelter shed. The roan pointed his ears at the cat, cocked his head, and backed a step. "Montana. At my grandfather's place. I'm going to have to stick around here for a little while."

"You sound great!" she said. "How are you doing?"

"I've been working on a colt—well, not exactly a colt. But see, the old man isn't well, and I promised to help him out for a couple of weeks. I'm sorry." The leggy cat advanced across the barnyard until the roan shied out of his way. The cat looked straight ahead as he passed.

After a pause, she said, "I'll call Mr. Kittredge and let him know you won't start work right away." Then, almost in the same breath, "Jack! The bone graft is working. I can walk!"

"And I can talk," I laughed.

"We'll be walking-talking fools," she answered, laughing too. The roan, slinking forward, one slow step at a time, was following the cat into some weeds.

I hung the dishpans on the wall behind the Monarch range, switched off the overhead light, and lit the Aladdin lamp on the table. Several days' worth of month-old papers lay piled in the kindling box. I pulled one out and scanned the headlines. The PLO had killed some children; the IRA had killed some bystanders; university students from Missoula had been arrested for protesting a Minuteman missile installation. One article caught my attention, a front-page story entitled BIG SKY ENDURES, DESPITE DARK CLOUDS, which told how removing sagebrush for an Arnold Palmer Associates golf course in the Gallatin Canyon had proven much tougher than planners first expected.

I glanced in at Harley, bent forward in his La-Z-Boy, absorbed in a *Star Trek* rerun. The last of the Charlie Russell cowboys, he had become a relic of his time, when dry grass had been good as gold, when men were ranked by the way they handled animals. I walked into the parlor and sat down beside him.

"What are you going to do for hay this winter, Harley?" I asked. "I see the barn is down."

"Barn's been down a couple years. This year I won't have to feed. We're going to ship the whole mess to Butte." He turned the sound down, so we could talk, but he kept his eyes on the spaceship, intent on Mr. Spock, who calmed an overwrought Captain Kirk. The *Enterprise* warp-sixed into lines of light and disappeared. Harley slapped his leg.

I remembered noticing that none of the hay meadows had been cut; the timothy, browned and gone to seed, stood bowed under its own slender weight.

"Lost fifty percent of my calves last winter, and it was an open year." Harley leaned back in the recliner. "I've run cattle fifty years, but I ain't going to keep on if I can't do it right." He looked over at me. "I'll settle on a time with Lonnie and Ted and Amy. You brace up those corrals. I got to line up trucks and inspectors too, and you need to learn that horse of yours to turn around inside of twenty acres."

I hadn't expected whirlies, just sitting there chewing the dog. But when they came I hung to my chair and tried to understand what Harley was saying. "There are other things too. Lots of changes around here. Dahls, I guess you knew, sold out while you were gone. Sold to a big outfit from out of state, land and cattle company called Tanners. They put some cows on the range for a couple seasons—way more than the grass could stand."

Harley rubbed his whiskered jaw. "When their cows got thin by fall they decided the range wasn't any good unless they had it all." Harley laughed, but his voice was mean. "So they started in hassling us who own land this side of Casey Creek."

Harley drew a line across his palm with his index finger. "That splits the summer range in half—besides ruining the country—and just generally puts the screws to the rest of us."

"But now that I'm back . . ." I said, feeling the dizziness easing off.

Harley snorted through his nose. "We expected you back *years* ago." He tapped his fingers on the recliner and watched Lieutenant O'Hura mince around the control room in her miniskirt.

"What about Ted and the Fords? And Amy?"

Shadows from the Aladdin's fluted chimney fluttered on the hewn ceiling beams. The *Enterprise* fired balls of energy into deep space. "Last July, Tanners parked a half dozen horse trailers at Rocker Gulch and twenty of those jailbirds they call cowboys took off in every direction, counting brands and taking pictures." The enemy craft burst into particles of phosphorescent light. "And since they claim to own over thirty sections out there now, and I only have two, they said—their *lawyers* said—I've got to get my cows off their grass."

"Don't their cattle graze your grass too? If this outfit wants them off, let 'em fence them off."

"That is just exactly what I told them." Harley turned in his chair and the thin leather squeaked under him. "But come to find out, they don't give a *damn* about grass. They're after *land*. Any land they can lay hands on, any by-Christ way they can."

"So let them shit in one hand and wish in the other."

Harley grinned. "Sure. Like you say, they got to fence my cattle out, if push comes to shove."

I sensed a punch line that I couldn't quite see. I fumbled with my makings, spilling the fine-cut tobacco on my knees.

"This new outfit ain't like dealing with Dahls. One day last spring I hear at Duncan's how some of their jailbirds had been in spouting off about how the range was going to get cleared one way or the other. Don't take much imagination to see how a few drunks with twenty-twos could put you out of the beef business in one moonlit night."

I pulled a fresh paper and started to roll another smoke.

"I'm not getting a range war started at my age. Seventy-five is too old for that nonsense."

Harley'd turned seventy-five when I started college. Somewhere back then he'd just drawn the line.

"Why don't you all get together? You and Schillings and Fords and fence your sections into one big unit?"

"You think about that a minute," Harley said, "and don't light that weed in here. I've got enough trouble with my wind without breathing your smoke."

"If you would all fence your ground," and as I said it, I saw it. Harley's punch line. "There isn't any water out there."

"You're pretty sharp," Harley said. "For a pilgrim."

I took the cigarette apart, folded a new paper, and began again, willing my hands steady. Each morning, I remembered, for a week in October, Harley and Summerfield and I would leave before dawn and lead our horses home in the dark. All day we rode the brushy bottoms and browngrass hills, bringing in one small bunch of grass-heavy cattle at a time. Harley hadn't turned seventy-five then, and he rode all day too, making sure we didn't run his cows, keeping an eye on saddle sores and hooves. What an outfit we were: Summer, usually riding a green-broke colt for somebody, Harley on the buckskin he called Chesterfield, and me, with one horse or another nobody else wanted, riding a saddle no one else would use. And Harley in charge, telling us how, when the country was young, he'd caught the bands of unbranded colts in the bald hills, and sold them branded within two weeks, broke to ride.

7

The corrals consisted of one large circular arena with pole gates opening east and west into runways, holding pens, and chutes. The big central corral had first been built by spiking rails to convenient trees in a rough circle. The rest had been added piecemeal over the years.

From the pole gate on the north side of the arena, two barbed wire fences fanned out through the trees for a quarter of a mile, making a hidden, funnel-shaped lane. Animals pressed down this narrowing trap entered the corral before they even saw it.

Most of the original trees had died and been cut down. Great fire-blackened pitch posts had been set in the ground between the stumps, but by now most of them had rotted off too and were held up only by the sagging rails.

I spent a couple days sawing up rails and cutting the rotten ends off the posts when they fell over. I dug new holes, planted the posts again, and tamped them tight. The soil was decomposed granite, good digging except for pine roots. My hands blistered on the iron fence bar, and my shoulders ached from its weight. *They'd leave in the moonlight. I was always up to watch them go. They would move out quiet, like shadows leading horses.*

The loading chute's main upright posts, which had been actual trees sawed off high, had rotted away too. The old chute swayed as I walked up the plank floor, but the sides, made of twelve-inch, rough-cut fir lumber, were still sound.

Harley's idea had been to shore up the weakest panels, set a few posts where needed, and get the gates to open enough to slick us by. But every time I pulled one thing loose, something somewhere else fell down. Harley finally couldn't stand watching from the house any longer. He backed a brand-new Chevy pickup from the shop, drove the three hundred yards to the barn, and looked around. "Won't have anything left pretty soon," he told me.

I shrugged, wiped the dry-rot dust from my sweating face, and sawed on. It seemed faster to replace the old than try to mend it, and besides, the work kept me from thinking about where I ought to be. *I'd help my mother milk, separate the cream, and clean the separator; I'd split enough kindling and stove wood for a week and pack a couple buckets of water up from the spring pipe. When I couldn't find anything else to do except get in the way, I'd climb a rock behind the barn and I'd listen and I'd wait.*

Smoke shut his logging operation down for a few days and showed up with his hay truck. He had the semi loaded with sixty green lodgepole rails, some fourteen-foot oak switch ties for gate and chute posts, and my Ford truck, chained down over the back wheels. He got out, looked around, shook his head, and said, "I thought you were in a hurry to get out of here."

I helped him shake the chain binders loose along the side of the semi trailer. "What's with my pickup?" I asked.

"Friday night," Smoke answered, the famous grin flashing on his handsome face. "'So come on wheels, take this boy to town.'"

"Another hot date?"

"You got that right, Jackson."

"Emmylou Harris she's not, Smoke."

We began carrying rails to where we'd need them. Smoke packed two at a time, the muscles beneath his T-shirt swelling, the sinews in his heavy arms corded and hard. I carried one at a time, in another direction.

When we'd unloaded the truck, Smoke brought a canvas water bag to where I sat on the railroad ties. He took a long drink, poured some water on the bandanna, and wiped his face.

"What I wouldn't give for a frosted mug of beer."

"Drink water," Smoke said, handing me the Desert Bag, "you'll piss just as far."

"Two more weeks and I'll be home, drinking beer and pissing foam."

Smoke cocked his head. I heard it too, the rolling, thudding impact of distant incoming, the detonations muted by the timber around us. I stood, felt myself tighten.

Smoke glanced at me. "That seismic outfit's working this way," he said. "Sounded like war up Crystal Creek yesterday."

I wet my face, neck, and arms with the dripping bandanna. "What's this land-and-cattle company deal?"

"Tanners? Oh, they're movers and shakers. Lots of money. They've been buying up land here and west of the Divide, which is funny, really, the way the cattle market has been."

The spaced detonations came again, and I could imagine the rounds landing in the woods, the yellow-white flashes tearing earth from under trees, the singing-hot slivers of iron meeting wood.

Smoke worked that day and the next, as steady and strong and enduring as a mountain mule. With drawknives we peeled two sides of each pole and took turns nailing them in place. The seven-inch, ring-shank spikes drove hard in the fire-tempered posts, but Smoke's late night in town didn't show in the way he swung a hammer.

The roan, loose in an acre of enclosed grass and weeds below the corral, stood at ease under a barn eave and watched our progress. I'd been riding him a couple hours each evening, and he was coming along. I'd even tried him once bareback, going up the meadows along the creek and past the old teepee rings, where the graves of my family lay in a sheltered park among some bull pine. Summer's grave had grassed over too, and except for the government stone, it looked like native prairie.

When Harley saw the new panels of fresh-peeled poles and the newly braced chute and the solid posts anchoring the gates, he acted like the whole design had been his idea.

"See?" he said to me. And nodding to Smoke he added, "Right, June?"

After making his point, Harley puffed up the slight incline inside the main arena, until he had to stop his inspection to catch his wind. He stood with his back to us, looking toward the fallen hay barn, as if planning something in that direction.

"Jesus, he looks rough," Smoke said under his breath. I held up a rail so he could spike it home. The shock of his hammer blows traveled up my arms and seemed to dead-end in my teeth. "We've got to be real careful he doesn't get hurt while we're working those cattle," he whispered. "Harley will want to get right in there with us, and he'll get mad if we try to keep him out of the way. Keep your eyes open. Watch out for him, so he don't get run over."

Harley turned and started toward us, pulling on a pair of yellow rag gloves as he walked. "So how's this girlfriend, Smoke?" I asked.

"She's a lot more fun than skidding logs, kid. You can't believe . . ."

Harley picked up the light end of a rail without waiting on us. Smoke took the other end and together they lifted it for me to nail.

"This is lodgepole," Harley said.

"Yeah, lodgepole," Smoke answered.

"Well, why didn't you cut fir? This crap won't last fifteen years!" With a sudden flash of anger, as if it had been work-

ing in him awhile, Harley faced my father and said: "And
why, for sweet Jesus' sake, don't you cut your damn hair?"

Sunday afternoon, as I was putting the finishing touches on
a squeeze chute gate, I heard a truck pull in at the house.
Amy and Annie Stevens climbed out and took some boxes
inside. The plank gate had swollen, and I planed wood from
the outer edge until it closed snug. We would clip the hair
from every brand when we brought in the cattle. We'd need
good luck and gates that worked to get it done. *You would
hear the men first, yelling and swearing. I'd double-check
the gates, run, and squeeze down a crack in the rocks out of
sight. They'd hit the flat this side of the Veracruz and you
could recognize each man's voice: Lester Cotkey, Uriel Reed,
the Skows and Flavvens, and Harley. It would get quiet
again when they entered the trees behind the bluff. Then all
at once, you heard them. The horses running.*
I put my tools away, brushed off my jeans, and emptied
my cuffs. The big corral looked like a different place now,
and I guessed it was. No unbranded colts ran the Bald Hills,
and the horsemen who had taken them were gone.
*When they came, they came fast, down through the rocks
and trees as hard as they could run—and they could run!—
raising dust that hid the riders behind. By then they knew
they were between fences, and when they saw that open gate,
they'd grunt and buck on through like they were home free.
They were horses like you don't see any more, every color
and cross, but almost all part workhorse. They were range
horses, and among them some dandies. My job was to close
the gate behind the last one without getting run down by the
riders. I was seven, eight, nine years old.*

II

8

Amy Stevens balanced a homemade cigarette on her quivering lower lip as I came into the kitchen. Her skin had yellowed from too much cortisone, but it seemed to match her orange-tinted hair, which, as Harley was fond of saying, came mostly from a bottle. Her gullied face seemed oddly Oriental when she smiled. "Good to see you, boy," she said, then bent back to mashing potatoes at the kitchen range, looking, as I had remembered her, forty-five going on seventy. Her hands were knotted with arthritis, her face by years of pain. She gave the spuds a beating, though, and from the smoldering butt on her lip, a liberal sprinkling of ash.

Her daughter Annie, auburn-haired and chesty, covered a basket of rolls with a dish towel and set them on the freshly laid table. She slipped her arms around me and gave me a hug. Older by ten years, she'd always treated me like a kid. I was surprised when she kissed me on the lips. "Good to have you back, Scooter," she said and touched the spatter of white hair on the side of my head. I kissed her back, and the others laughed, as if the whole deal had been planned.

"You young ones tear yourselves apart now, so we can eat," her mother said, and we sat down at the table together, neighbors who were almost family. By way of grace, Harley said, "We got our corrals ready. How about yours?"

"They're plenty good enough," Amy said, answering his challenging eye, "to hold your stuff."

It was supposed to be a welcome-home dinner, but the main idea was to figure who would do what when we went out after the cattle. Annie and Smoke and I would ride. Harley and Amy would drive pickups, open and close gates, and bring meals out as needed. We would cut Tanners' and Schillings' and Ford's animals in the hills, but since for convenience we'd bunch some of Amy's registered Angus at Harley's and some of his animals at her place, they felt it necessary to argue strategies.

By the time I cut the pie, Harley and Amy had traded hot words, and Annie—probably the best rider among us—had taken sides against everybody. When the pie was gone, Smoke, who hadn't had much to say while he ate, finally spoke up. "We'll take the ones closest to Amy's to her place and bring the rest here. Then we'll truck Harley's animals from both places and take Amy's holdovers home."

Harley rough-locked his eyebrows, Amy glared at Harley, and it was settled.

Annie set a six-pack of Duck beer on the table. Smoke had a cup of coffee and mentioned a pair of matched Percherons he had his eye on in Wolf Creek. I snapped open a can of beer and took a long pull. Under the table, I felt Annie's leg bump mine. When I'd been in grade school, Annie had been the town punch in two towns at once. Summerfield told me about that while we were picking bales one August. We were plenty young, and we laughed, swinging the bales onto a chaff-hot flatbed, dreaming shade and Annie's cool thighs. Like her mother, Annie had never married, and while she was a catch colt, nobody I knew ever held it against her.

Amy rubbed the back of one hand gently, then the other. "This goddamned range deal," she said. "I always leave my stuff out until Thanksgiving. You know that. Besides, I've only got a hundred and sixty acres outside my wire, and even fenced that wouldn't do me much good."

"Leave 'em out there then," Harley said.

Amy shook her head no. "If we'd all stuck together," she said. "That would be different."

"Say. I saw Wes Lindsay on my way up this morning," Smoke interjected, in what looked like a deliberate move to cut off more arguing at the pass. "He's drilling on the Harris place."

Although a clapboard house still stood beside the gash of quarry, no one in my time had lived there. Amy's sodbuster folks had farmed the place for a while—after Harris took his limerock money back east—but they hadn't lasted long.

"Some contractor bought it, Lindsay says. Wants to parcel it up if they get water."

Annie popped a second beer and belched softly into her callused palm.

"He's down four hundred feet. Solid limerock. Hasn't even hit mud yet, and this is the second hole."

"I could have told them that," Harley said.

Amy raised her eyes toward the ceiling. "You don't need to tell *me*, Harlan. I saw it so hot down there you'd faint on the way to the shitter."

"Eighteen dollars a foot, Lindsay says."

"And they want to subdivide it?" Annie asked. "I wonder how they feel about rattlesnakes?"

"Brimstone Estates," Harley said and slapped his leg. "Free canteen and pet reptiles with each lot." Tickled by the idea, Harley laughed until a fit of coughing cut him short.

"I tried to tell you there'd be trouble last spring, Harlan, when we first spotted those surveyors out there," Amy snapped. "They're running us off our grass, and you're laughing about it!"

Harley cut his watering eyes to Amy and straightened in his chair. "Surveying don't put water in the ground. Your folks hauled their water. Maybe this guy will too."

Annie began to clear the table, and I helped her stack the plates. Harley and Amy wrangled on, and Smoke glanced from his pocket watch to me as he stood. "I'll be here early," he said. "Be ready to go at first light."

"I understand Mr. Smoke has a pretty active nightlife these days," Annie whispered with a light in her eye.

"I'm going to have to cut 'er off, though," Smoke grinned. "Until we get these precious thirty-five-cent cows back home."

I closed the door to my room and lit a kerosene lamp I'd found and filled in the oil house. The overhead electric bulb was just too bright for anything but reading. After laying out some clean clothes, I sat down on Summer's weight bench and kicked off my boots. A bar, loaded with weights, lay in the forked uprights of the bench. I added up the iron plates to two hundred and sixty-five pounds and remembered once seeing Summer ride at the Townsend rodeo. He'd drawn a black bull called Short Stack, which had only been covered once that year. Summer not only rode him, he outmuscled him. Or so it looked from the chutes.

I unbolted the keepers on the end of the bar and removed a hundred pounds, patted both hands on the rosin sock, and lay down beneath the weights. I only managed to lift it once, so I removed a twenty-pound plate from each side and did three sets of six presses.

Between sets, I put together a bar for curls and a short bar for chest lifts and extensions. As I sweated through the workout I remembered Summer changing the weights and talking to himself, urging himself on to the best he could give, pushing himself the way he'd often pushed me, toward winning.

I tried it as I began doing curls, imitating at first, the way I remembered his monologues running: "Uhh! Here he comes; huh! out of chute number three; huh! on the horse called; uhh! Sister's Revenge." And for a moment I was there, outside my room, outside myself, grunting and pulling, my knees flying in a clean, machinelike rhythm and only three seconds into the ride I knew I had him covered. When the pickup man dropped me running, out of the path of the still bucking horse, I picked up my hat and waved at the crowd. That first show—after we teamed up at Williams Lake—I placed in the money. The next two, both indoor affairs, I won and placed again in the fourth. Men I didn't know slapped me on the back behind the chutes while I waited for my little barrel-racing partner to finish her ride.

I stopped. My hands and arms burned; I'd lost count and done too many. But I wanted it; I wanted it again bad, so I curled the bar one last time.

9

Harley hadn't yet stirred upstairs when I heard tires crunching the frost-hard dirt in the dark yard. Working by the gentle light of the Aladdin, I broke a half dozen eggs in a bowl, drained grease from the snapping bacon, and poured two cups of coffee. As I turned bread, toasting on a wire screen above the wavering surface of the range, I heard the tailgate open on the stock truck and the halting, hollow-sounding steps of Smoke's Walker unloading.

Smoke came in slapping his hands and wiping his nose. "Lactated titters! Cold as a virgin girl's heart." He hung his batwing chaps to warm behind the range, wrapped his heavy hands around a smoking mug of coffee, and glanced up at the ceiling. I shook my head no.

A blue haze of bacon smoke hung above the stove as I slopped eggs into a cast-iron pan, dumped in grated cheese, and stirred fast. When they thickened, I divided the eggs onto plates and pulled a pan of hash browns from the warming oven over the range. Smoke looked wide awake and expectant as he straddled a chair at the table. "Smells pretty good for a hillbilly. Where'd you learn to cook like this?"

"I had a little apartment off post in Lawton, after I became an instructor. Breakfast was my specialty."

"One WAC, over easy?"

"Too greasy. Mostly poached the WACs."

He put his face over his food and ate without looking up.

When he paused for a gulp of coffee, he said, "We'll pick up Annie and start on the west end. Work north and east today and tomorrow. Your horse ready?"

"Green as grass. He ever been up close to a cow before?" Smoke grunted. "I'll help you get him started. Did you have any trouble getting on him?"

"Nothing to it," I said, rising to get more potatoes. "He didn't have a buck in him."

For a moment Smoke stared at me over his raised cup. "That's right," he said, "and I'm Dolly Parton." For the first time since I'd come back, we smiled together.

Upstairs, we heard Harley coughing and clomping along the hall. As his boots appeared at the top of the steps, his dry voice rustled down. He was singing: "Chickery chic, cha la cha la, olly ca bolli ca, can't you see?"

After breakfast, I caught the roan and led him to the house. Smoke dragged Summerfield's roping saddle from the front seat of his truck and handed it to me. It was still like new, except for a layer of dust hiding the glossy finish. "Keep it, kid," he said. "No use riding that ass-breaker of yours."

"He drove grain trucks for Simpson to buy it."

"Yeah."

"Remember? He was too young to get a license, but he bulled those grain trucks that whole harvest anyway."

"Yeah. I remember. Take good care of it." Smoke had started my brother as a team roping partner. As soon as he was old enough, Summer moved up to bulls. That had left Smoke without a partner, and since I couldn't catch a calf with a net under pressure, he just retired. It occurred to me then that Summer and I had deserted both Harley and Smoke more often than we'd intended. More often than they deserved.

We saddled the horses in the light of the open shop door. The roan kept stepping sideways as I worked on him, wanting to show off for Smoke's bay, a Morgan-Walker cross, who stood with his nose touching the shop wall, his eyes almost closed. Summer and I had laughed when Smoke brought him home, but the first day we rode together, we stopped laughing. Half asleep, the Walker could outdistance any horse around, in any kind of country. He could move, and he had all the bottom in the world.

We led them the first three hundred yards to the red gate, tightened our cinches, and walked them out another couple hundred feet. Smoke mounted and his Walker took off in the swinging, ground-eating stride that I knew would be as long and steady that evening as it was right then. I tied my halter lead to the lariat keeper on the pommel, cheeked the roan around, and stepped aboard. He jumped into a bone-jarring trot, all springs and nonsense again, and shook his head like he might fire up when I eased him back with the antique curb bit Harley insisted I use.

Without discussing it, we rode twenty yards apart through the absolute darkness of the woods and out onto the open, starlit prairie. Iridescent green and blue streaks of Peacock copper–colored light climbed the eastern sky. My arms and shoulders ached from my session with Summer's weights; I could feel frost falling cleanly against my hands and face.

We left the wire gate open in the boundary fence beside Harley's pole cattle guard. Then, beyond his fence, but still upon his land, we rode west to the edge of a long, grassy ridge called Cutler Hill. In the growing light we could see the three-mile-long trough between the timbered thrust of Skihi peak and the swelling, treeless expanse of the bald hills toward Helena.

We stopped the horses and let them blow. From where we sat, we could see only two lights in fifteen square miles: one at the old Cutler place directly below, and one at Amy's, a couple miles to the west. The rest of that open and roadless land had been as free as the night for us to use.

Through it all ran a twisting, brush-covered ditch called

Casey Creek. Dredged in a couple places to make water holes, Casey supplied each spring the only water between the unpredictable seeps at the Big Indian Mine west of Amy's and the pond in Flavven's meadow to the east of Harley's. But by now, Casey Creek had been dry along most of its course for several months.

"The old man was full of fire this morning," Smoke said. "Must be your cooking."

"My cooking didn't have anything to do with him dragging out his duster and spurs."

"Pretty sharp. Acting like he might be called on to ride in a pinch."

"How long do you figure this will take, Smoke?"

"With no wrecks, four or five days. You ought to be able to cut loose in a week, easy. You feeling all right?"

"You bet. But what's going to happen to Harley after I leave?"

"I might have to move him down to the valley with me. We'll see."

Smoke's bay yawned and shook his head, jingling his snaffle snaps. He chewed at something he found in his back teeth and waited for the long walk to begin. I felt an old excitement in my chest, a tightness and urgency like the buck fever that had plagued me when Smoke first took me deer hunting. I'd been, I remembered, so afraid of messing up in front of him then that it wasn't until Summer and I hunted together that I began to shoot well.

"Close as I can figure, Harley's got a hundred and sixty—odd cows, plus around seventy coming two-year-olds—both heifers and steers. Six old bulls with weight-turned horns, and fifty or sixty unbranded calves. They'll be trouble, the calves. They've never been touched."

"Unbranded?"

"Didn't bring his cows in last year." Smoke popped the lid on his snuff can with his knuckles and twisted it open. "I was trucking hay from my place to Miles City. Harley hadn't put up any hay and wouldn't be bothered hiring winter help, so he just left them out."

"No wonder he lost half his calves."

"He lost more than that. It gave this new outfit, Tanners, just the leverage they needed to sic their lawyers on him."

The roan lifted his head and pointed his ears. We looked too, and saw a coyote trot across the county road below, his head high and watchful in the tall grass.

"Old Amy's the one this range deal is going to bust. You can't buy feed and hire pasture too, even with registered stuff like hers. The money just isn't there come payday. Not having this pasture will ruin her, and it'll make everybody else, except maybe Ted, marginal."

The coyote passed through a growth of young pine now reclaiming a deserted field the old man named Cutler cleared even before Harley's folks had come to homestead. Cutler had sold horses to the army, and he'd taught Harley much of what he knew about wrangling. Although he'd been dead over fifty years, his place and one hill kept his name. My father and I started down the ridge, looking out across the country as a new day came upon the land.

10

In the distance, Annie looked like a man in her blanket coat and Scotch cap as she led her Appaloosa from the timber to meet us. She mounted like a man too, lots surer than most.

"You watch that roan around her mare," Smoke said. "No telling when he was cut or what he'll pull."

Annie's mare had a bow in her neck and a hump in her back, but Annie rode with one hand in her coat pocket, as if she didn't notice. "So how are things over at the granite ghetto?" she asked, her eyes happy above her upturned coat collar. She looked the roan over as we moved out, opening her mouth to say something, then changing her mind.

A half hour later we fell wordlessly into old patterns when we found the first bunch of bedded cattle. Annie and Smoke circled them, pointing now and then to animals they wanted. Annie worked the inside, gradually cutting singles and pairs out to Smoke, who eased them away from the main group. The Walker swung side-to-side, never breaking into a trot, never seeming to hurry, yet always alert and always there.

When they had cut six head, I rode in beside Smoke and reined my roan to face the staring animals. The cattle bunched and stood facing us until a yearling, bold and curious, took a few tentative steps ahead. The roan backed up. I touched him with the spurs. "We're supposed to chase *them*," I told him, "not run and hide." I touched him again,

a little harder, and he jumped. The calf spun and the rest
turned with him down the hill. Three abreast we headed the
heavy-bellied cattle for Amy's back gate. They ran and
walked, bobbing their heads, and shitting green down their
tails as they went. In the early quiet, we could hear the
clacking of their hoof joints above the rumbling of our
horses' guts.

We let the cattle walk, bunched and nervous, to the edge
of the timber, then pushed them the last couple hundred
yards at a trot. Annie followed the cattle through the main
corral, pushed them into a holding pen, and hooked a board
gate behind them. As she turned her mare toward us, my
roan snorted and reared, shying off to my left.

"Pretty goosey, huh?" Annie said, coming alongside.

I gave him his head and he stepped out, stopped, and
jumped again. "Maybe girls make him foolish, I don't
know."

"Uh-huh. You let me know when he gets over that,
Scooter." Annie tucked her chin back in her collar and rode
on, smiling to herself. Smoke dropped back to take a squirt,
and for the time being we rode without talking. Then, surprising myself, I said, "I'm going to ride again, Annie. Jackson's the name, and rodeo's my game."

She glanced at me like I'd just landed from Krypton.
"Well, that's good. You were doing real fine there for a
while."

"Yes, ma'am. Got a job lined up in God's country, a lady
friend, and by next spring I'll be back in shape."

"Seems I've heard about this lady friend of yours, Scooter.
Didn't she get busted up pretty bad?"

"She's got a plastic hip, and I've got a plate in my head.
Make a winning combination for sure."

"Sounds like true love," Annie answered, looking a little
bored.

"She'd enjoy this. Riding early and all. You'd like her,
Annie," I said. "She's a lot like you."

We fanned out onto separate ridges, climbing, as we worked north, toward Helena. We checked the brushy draws twisting below, yet from time to time we were able to see each other.

Near the top of the bald hills, the ridges ran together in clusters of wind-tortured limber pine that grew bent east as if a hard wind still blew. Cattle had walked out beds among the trees during the summer, carpeting the ground with a couple inches of dry manure. Red and black calves disappeared in the timber ahead, and as we trotted after them, I could hear Annie, off in the trees, saying to Smoke: "So the Mexican says, 'But Padre, if God didn't want man to eat pussy, why did He make it look so much like a taco?'"

"They told me they're locating a road over there," Amy said, clattering lunch dishes and empty pop cans into a cardboard box on the tailgate of her Chevy Apache. She scowled at Harley, who, glassing the country to the east of us, didn't answer.

"They claimed it would cross below the pond and go up Harris Hill toward those yellow pine on top."

"Roads usually go some*place*," Harley said. "Besides, it looks like they're snoozing to me."

"How do you know they won't cross your ground?"

"Too far north." One thing about Harley: he knew where original corner stones were located in a considerable chunk of country. On the other hand, he was pretty closemouthed about where some of them were.

"It wouldn't hurt to talk to them, Harlan."

"They know where I live," Harley answered, the binoculars still hiding his eyes.

Smoke and Annie and I watched the old folks from a rock outcropping where we'd eaten. A road up Harris Hill seemed a remote idea, an improbable notion. Like Harley said, roads usually went some*place,* and there was nothing on Harris Hill, except grass and game trails. I didn't for a moment believe it would happen.

Amy poured coffee from a thermos jug the size of a 105 round. "I don't see what business they have driving all over off the road like that."

"Looks like lots of folks with no business out here are here anyway." Smoke shaded his deep-set eyes and watched as a second pickup climbed toward the distant survey crew.

"This isn't anything new, you know." Harley lowered the glasses and sat down on the tailgate. He reached one long hand toward the horizon and swept the country. "Land locators were thick as ticks when we first came. Everybody was staking out a quarter then, water or no water, greedy for free land."

I watched a red-tailed hawk work a thermal above some frost-yellowed aspen on Skihi, watched until he picked up a current of wind and drifted out of sight behind the mountain. But on the far side of the mountain, like a movie trick, a helicopter appeared instead of the hawk.

"They're just coming like that again is all, only there will be more this time. Hell! There were still Indians in the hills then, instead of pickups and power lines. When *I* was a kid, the army had a big camp of 'em right where that fancy motel this side of town is now. Mounted soldiers kept them poor devils out on that flat all winter. Fed 'em on tripes from the stinkin' slaughterhouse. Miserable. We were living in a tent then too, but at least we had a tin stove and good groceries."

I could see something swinging below the copter, although distance made the cable hard to see.

Harley narrowed his eyes. "I remember one morning I was taking a team and wagon through Butcherknife, headed for town. I came around a corner down in the narrows, and standing on the trail up ahead was the poorest excuse for an

Indian you ever saw. Skinny, had on a pair of leggins and a suit coat with no sleeves. Sucker had a rock in one hand the size of a horseshoe."

"When was all this?" Annie asked, tucking in her shirt as she returned from some bushes.

"When I was a kid. Anyway, I figured he was going to try and bust me with the rock, maybe take my dad's team. I had a rolling block thirty-eight–forty-four that had been shot smooth leaning against one knee—might as well have been throwing rocks myself—so I just kept those horses moving. Rascal tagged along behind the wagon 'til I came to his camp. Had some half-rotten hides hung on poles for shelter, and the ugliest woman I *ever* saw, except'n' present company, maybe, cooking some stuff over a smudge."

Annie poked Amy and laughed, but Amy acted like she hadn't heard.

"So what did you do, Harley?" I asked.

"Why, I kept going," he answered, watching Amy from the corner of his eye. "What would *you* do?"

I shrugged, trying to picture myself at that age in the same fix.

"He didn't want me molesting his camp was all. He looked like he'd about been molested long enough. Next time I came through, though, they were gone."

"We better get gone too," Smoke said, "if we're going to make it home by dark."

Harley faced the hills that had been so good to him in his youth, and what he saw left a thin smile on his weatherworn face. "I brought along some fresh meat and hard bread that second trip," he said quietly, "but they'd already moved on."

II

For the next two days we rode the dry hills, picking up scattered bunches of cattle and cutting out the strays. Harley's unbranded spring calves proved to be as bad as Smoke had said. Wild as deer, they ran bug-eyed into thickets of chokecherry and juniper so thick a man on foot couldn't follow. We'd move on and circle back later, flushing them like pheasants across open ground in the general direction of home.

On the second afternoon we used the corrals at the abandoned Martinez Ranch to hold thirty head overnight. Joe Martinez had raised workhorses, and he'd broken famous teams to harness. Harley pronounced his name Marteenz, and spoke of him with respect. I could barely remember the man, and wondered what had happened to the gangly kid who'd once come with Harley to see Joe's horses, wondered why no one had moved into Joe's house or made use of his barns in the years since he died, wondered why, when his family had scattered, the young ones turned so wild.

In three days we managed to clear most of the bald hills, and the cattle, penned at random in Amy's corrals, raised a steady sad noise: cows bawled for calves they couldn't find, calves bawled for cows they couldn't reach, bulls raged and pawed dirt onto their backs, and the big steers moaned and bellowed for no good reason except perhaps the general calamity of their lives.

.   .   .

"At least you had a quiet night," Amy said as she lugged the thermos on her morning coffee round. She ran her bent fingers through her bright, unruly hair and glared at Smoke. "They raised steady hell here, I'll tell you."

Smoke stood and put one heavy arm around Amy's slender waist. "And what makes you think I had a quiet night?" he asked, giving her a gentle squeeze.

We ran a dozen head into the chute at a time, inoculating Amy's yearlings for shipping fever and blackleg, shooting growth pellets into the steer calves, replacing missing ear tags, and dusting each animal for lice. Then we turned her Angus out to the meadows below her house, and that afternoon began working Harley's Herefords. Smoke pushed them up from behind, while Annie and I clipped away the rich, red hair high on each left haunch until we could see, or at least feel, the welted outline of the Lazy-H-Triangle. We made good time until Harley showed up and insisted on checking each animal himself. Even so, we'd finished by the time the cattle inspector came to make out the shipping papers.

The next morning—after Honest Barry Kitterman's overloaded semi creaked down the county road from Amy's, weighted with the first of Harley's cattle to go—we rode cross-country to the Interstate interchange at Helena. We brought every animal we could find as we came, planning to sort them later at the upper dredge pond. By early afternoon we were drowsy with sun, riding warm in our shirt sleeves, brushing seventy-some sleepy cows up a long grassy slope. I pulled my hat down against the sun, smiling to myself at how the roan would stack up with the fancy barrel-racing horses the girl in Canada rode. He was still green, but he liked to work, managing each day to learn something new; he was hot and flashy and becoming sure of me. He'd hold his own with her quarterhorses, I decided, and relaxed in the rhythm of his steps, tickled by the idea of watching her watch him. My body ached from the hours of riding and the workouts with Summer's weights, and in my sore-muscled sleep, I dreamed the roan running.

I snapped awake, realizing that he was running, running sideways and trying to rear. A helicopter hovered down the grassy hill above the milling cattle, flying a hundred yards or so above the ground, a pallet swinging on a cable from one skid. The rotor noise doubled as another chopper appeared behind the first; together, they came down the ridge like huge, brightly colored wasps, beating up vortices of dust and chopped grass that raced along the ridge and caught us.

Cattle ran past, some brushing the horse, who bucked once, almost fell, and hesitated. I looked around for the others. Annie had one hand on her saddle horn, riding her pitching mare in a tight circle. As the roan swung his ass uphill, I saw Smoke's Walker going down, saw Smoke for an instant trying to step off as the bay turned over. And then all I could see was running cattle dispersing around the roan, who took off wide open with them down the rocky hillside we'd just labored up.

I lost my hat and the right-side stirrup. The lead helicopter, directly above us, felt like it was going to land on my back, and from the corner of my eye, I saw the cable swinging toward us. Sand and chaff stung my face as I hauled back on the lines. The roan reared and lunged ahead, panicking as I panicked. I threw the right rein up along the horse's neck, pulled his face around, took a dally on the horn, and, holding it with both hands, stepped off and leaned out away from him. He plowed on a couple of lunging strides, looking back over his shoulder, until finally overbalanced by my weight and unable to see, he piled up and rolled as I tried to jump clear. I hit on my back and wasn't sure for a few seconds where I was. As in a dream, I saw a field gun rise in a yellow-white ball of light, felt a freight train—like concussion hit my face. Ragged pieces of torn gunner's shields sliced by, warbling end over end through the air around me, cutting down my trainees like weeds. And my buddy Garrett looking so surprised. . . .

We slid to a stop in the rocky soil, and I managed to run on my knees far enough to fall on the roan's neck. We lay there panting and scared, fighting each other in the hammering dust devils and flying sand, sliding inch by inch downhill, until the second helicopter thudded past. The horse pawed at me with his front feet. I hung onto him and kept his head down until the indifferent choppers gained altitude and disappeared into silent dots.

I knelt beside Smoke in the hot shade of a young bull pine where we had dragged him to wait, and watched as Annie rode away. Smoke had sweated his shirt through, front and back; his contorted face glistened as he opened his eyes and ran his tongue over his dry lips. "If I get cross hairs on those sonsabitches, I'm going to ruin their whole day," he said.

"Do you think it's broken, Smoke?"

"No. I know it's broken."

"Annie'll be back with help pretty soon." I stood and walked to the horses, tied in the shade of another pine. The roan had lost some hair on his left shoulder, foreleg, and hip, but he seemed sound. The fall had scuffed up Summer's saddle though, tearing the fancy tooling on the skirts and jockeys, and gouging the left side of the swells. The rawhide-wrapped wooden stirrup hadn't broken, and I knew he'd be tender in the ribs for a few days. As I rolled off the saddle, I remembered Smoke's disgust with me when, years before, he'd tried to teach me to hunt elk. "You want to daydream, you might as well stay home," he finally said. And he'd been right; then, like now, I never seemed ready when the action started. That had been my mistake on the range at Fort Sill that day too, a mistake I would carry with shame to my grave. Maybe there was nothing I could have done about the helicopters, but being awake sure wouldn't have hurt.

I noticed Smoke's Walker, hanging his head as if embarrassed. Of the three horses, he'd been the long shot to fall. But it was a fluke that meant I'd have to get a grip on what was happening around me, because my mistakes, it seemed, always hurt others more than they ever hurt me.

I lifted Smoke by the shoulders and slid the saddle pad under his back. "Sweet mother-of-pearl," he said through clenched teeth; his skintight face—exposed by the way he tied back his hair—looked as rigid and pale as if carved from horn.

I held my hat to shade his face, wishing one of us had carried a canteen. Smoke lay sweating and silent until we heard a vehicle on the abandoned dirt road just below. Smoke turned his head toward the sound. "Oh, great," he said, sounding beat.

Harley spotted us and bounced his pickup across the flat and up the hill toward us. "Listen," Smoke touched my arm. "You call Sandy for me when we get to town. Tell her I can't make it tonight."

I walked to Harley's truck and told him about the wreck. He got a stick from the back of the truck and, leaning upon it, headed for Smoke. I watched for flashing lights, actually able to see part of Saint Peter's Hospital not two miles away. Slow minutes passed. When finally the red and blue lights appeared at the edge of town, I turned back to my father and grandfather.

". . . haven't seen a horse thrown like that since you took on that stud for Clyde Burgess that time," Smoke was saying.

"That right?" Harley asked, tilting his head back until his jaw was horizontal.

"Quite a show, Dad. The kid and the horse going down, those choppers sitting right there on 'em, and"—Smoke tried to laugh—"the kid just hugging that roan to death."

"Now, that stud . . ." Harley said. "Blazefaced sorrel with white stocking feet?" When Smoke didn't answer, we looked down and saw that he'd passed out again.

12

The smell stopped me at first. I turned around and walked back into the evening air, remembering as I went that sweet odor of hospitals, a scent one half alcohol, one half pain. I lit a cigarette, holding the new issue of *Field & Stream* I'd brought for Smoke rolled under one arm. Below the hospital, the Helena valley glittered with yard lights; the soft hum of a town bedding down vibrated around me. In the dusk it could have been anywhere I'd ever been in the West, any of the dozens of towns stalking out across the fields.

The receptionist remembered the name and directed me toward Smoke's room. I walked long corridors, glancing into rooms where people lay watching TV, cut off for the moment, or forever, from life.

Smoke sat propped on pillows on the inclined bed, writing in the pale gray light of the room, making notes on a small pad. He had an IV in one arm, and the elevated cast showed beneath the thin blanket covering his legs. I handed him the magazine. On the cover, a bull elk bugled a challenge to the mountains above him, hearing, perhaps, the enraged answer of his echo. Smoke grinned and smoothed the magazine on his good leg. "How'd you make out today?" he asked, his eyes lingering on the bull.

I leaned against the wall and studied his muscled arms, exposed by the hospital gown. "We got one bunch as far as Bell's cabin and lost them in the brush." There wasn't a building, really, at Bell's cabin, just a few scattered boards hidden by underbrush and a lilac bush that bloomed each June. Like many homesteaders, Bell had come and gone so long ago that only his name remained.

"I've done that myself. You have to keep 'em back in the hills until you hit Rocker Gulch. Either that or take them around Harris Hill."

"I tried to get hold of the helicopter people on the phone before Harley did. Left a message on their answering machine."

"I've got a little message I'm going to deliver in person, just as soon as I get out of here. I got the number off the one that ran us down." For a man with an eighth-grade education, Smoke had quite a head for numbers. If he called someone once on the telephone or saw a license plate one time, that number was his. I'd seen him accurately scale a standing tree into board feet and board feet into dollars in his head, and make almost instant cents-per-pound multiplications on truckloads of cattle. I had three and a half years of college and used a pencil.

"Don't do it," I said. "You've got everything to lose and nothing to gain, and I've got enough trouble right now."

"Here. You're going to have to take charge up there for now." Smoke handed me the notes he'd made. Pointing to each, he ran down the list. "Be sure to call Ray. Ask him to board my team and hang that harness until one of us can get up there to haul them home. Call the kid who was cutting for me, and tell him he's out of a job. And have the flower shop send a dozen roses to this address. Red ones."

"You've got a phone right there."

"You do it. I'm doped half the time, hurting the rest. You can pull more weight for a while. The guy who set my leg says two weeks in here minimum. And be sure to lock the buildings and front gate at my place. Leave a light on in the house and the radio going in the shop. Lots of rip-off artists prowling the back roads these days."

"Maybe you ought to think about hiring some help. You're going to be laid up for a while."

Smoke hit me with his eyes. "Maybe you should think about paying some old debts," he answered. "Especially to Harley, while you've still got the chance."

The El Camino rolled into a slot between two parked cars as I walked toward Harley's pickup. The engine raced, idled, and died with a clatter of cam and piston rods. A woman stepped out. Slim, dressed in white pants and a leather jacket, she held the door a moment before slamming it. I watched Sandy Martinez walk toward me, her heels snapping on the sidewalk with each confident stride, her hands hidden deep in the slit pockets of her coat.

"Hey, man," she said, recognizing me. "How's the old guy doing?"

"Flat-backing it right now. I stayed till they ran me off." Sandy's head made a little jerk. She stopped and looked up at me. "You could sneak in for a minute, but he's asleep."

She swayed, touching me for an instant with her shoulder. "Visiting hours over, huh?" Running her eyes over me, she seemed to come to a decision. Her sharp-featured face brightened, she swung back toward the parking lot, and took my arm. "Let's get high," she said.

At her El Camino I slipped loose. "I can't right now."

"Sure you can. I've got some bad shit. Fuck you up, and I mean *fuck* you up, too. Looks like you could use all of that you can get." She slipped one hand inside my jacket. "No bullshit, man. Am I wrong?" She shivered, and as if by magic, the tremor rippled down her lean body. She laughed a thin, private laugh, her teeth flashing bright in her shadow-halved face. "Come on, 'The One Who's Not,' let's rip."

The nights in the ward at Fitzsimmons, the hours of listening to coughs and cries in the night, and the hunger of months of waiting came on me in a rush. "Maybe I'll swing by later. What's your address?"

She told me, giving me a stoned-in-detail plan of her apartment building while tracing a design on my belt buckle with one thin finger.

"Take a rain check and look in on Smoke," I said and walked away, not daring to look back. If I was going to start repaying Harley for raising me, I figured I'd need all the sleep I could get.

13

Ted Schillings, two of his blond, teenage sons, Lonnie Ford, and Annie met me above the dredge pond at the foot of Cutler Hill. We rode down Casey Creek three abreast, past Bell's cabin, discussing Smoke's fall and what needed to be done to finish up. The cattle Annie and I had lost the day before grazed above us on the ridges to the west. We left them alone, hoping to pick them up on our way back. Without a word, the lead went to Ted in Smoke's absence. He was the eldest, a man of sound judgment, and without thinking we all trusted his experience.

Lonnie and I rode side by side for a while, quiet in the morning chill. His fine dark features reminded me of handsome white actors who used to play Indian chiefs in grade B Westerns. Long-legged and well built, he rode with strength and grace. For several years, Harley had leased their place for fall pasture, and Lonnie and I had spent a lot of afternoons head-and-heel-roping Harley's spring calves. Harley never caught us, although he'd sometimes remark on how wild his calves were when we took them home. Not long after I left home, there was the siege at Wounded Knee, and the teepee began to appear at Lonnie's each summer.

We split up beyond a new, open-pit limerock quarry near the old Hirsch place, Annie and I riding north toward Helena, Ted and his boys and Lonnie swinging south to cover the Harris place and Flavven's meadows, where cattle gathered each day at water.

72

By three o'clock, Annie and I had picked up three dozen cows and calves. We met the Schillings and Lonnie coming from the upper end of Flavven's, trailing well over a hundred head. We joined our bands and pushed them through the hills, skirting the new quarry and picking up bunches of stragglers on the way. By following a wide ditch Chinese miners had dug nearly a century before, we wound our way along the foothills above Casey Creek. The old ditch had grassed over; smooth-bottomed and shallow, it made a good, single-file trail. Ted's sons fanned out on buffalo trails contouring our flanks, adding the strays of the day before as we went.

I noticed tall, stemmy weeds growing in the poorer soil along the ridges. Each plant contained dozens of open seedpods that rattled in the light wind we faced. I couldn't remember ever seeing the plant before and asked Ted what it was.

"Knapweed," he answered. "Just hit this country a couple years ago. Each plant can produce a hundred thousand seeds, and the roots put a chemical into the ground that kills off the native grass. Quite an outfit. It outpopulates everything else in an area and poisons the soil against competitors. It's completely taken over some valleys west of the Divide. Ruined the pasture, put some folks right out of business."

From Rocker Gulch, we let the cattle run toward the smell of water at the dredge pond. Although we couldn't see it yet, we knew that's where they'd head; Casey Creek, below the water hole, had been dusty dry for at least two months.

As we rode up onto the big flat, we saw the cows lined out for a quarter mile ahead, trailing dust as they trotted toward water. And we saw two pickups, parked as if waiting for us, beside the muddy rim of the pond. One was Harley's, the other I didn't recognize.

The cattle hesitated at the outer edge of the sloping mud

flats, milling and bunching and turning back bawling. As we got closer, I saw fence posts and the gleam of new barbed wire circling the reservoir. Harley was talking to someone, waving one arm toward the cattle. I put the roan into a trot.

Cattle surrounded both trucks as I stepped down, the last to arrive pushing forward as the first turned along the new wire. Several men in work clothes faced Harley, whose shouted words were lost in the bellowing of the cattle. Dust rose and hung in the air, tasting, even dried, of the sour bog it had been that spring. Harley, I noticed, held a heavy-handled fencing tool in one hand.

I shook my halter rope loose and pulled the bridle off the roan. As I tied him to Harley's front bumper, I heard Harley shout, "Well, how the hell are you going to water *your* stock?" I started over to collect him, hearing him say, as I got closer, "That's rich! You people cry about our cattle, and when we come out to get them, you say we're trespassing." The man Harley was talking to stood grinning, his thumbs in the pockets of his jeans. He was flanked by four younger fellows, who looked like they'd put in a long day and wanted to head for home.

The cattle lined the bright wire, looking through the strands at the scummy water below, bawling long and loud. I walked through them until I got to Harley and asked him what was going on.

"Goddamn! Can't you *see?*" he shouted. The man I took to be the foreman glanced at me, the grin on his sunburned face widening as he watched Harley choke on the rising dust.

"Listen," I said to him. "We've got to fill these cows up before we can move them anywhere. Soon as we sort them, we'll get ours out of here. Where's the gate?"

"No gate, Sport," he said. "Just stay the hell away from that fence." He wore, I noticed when he laughed in my face, a brand-new brown Resistal hat that was fast turning gray.

Harley held up his fencing tool. "We're gonna fix that,

right now," he said. In his eyes I saw an anger I'd forgotten, an anger which was, while it lasted, a force that cut a swath through opposition. Harley pushed his way toward the fence in the circling cattle as if he were walking through grazing sheep. The man took off after him. I glanced at the workers, who looked bone tired and hot. One met my eyes and shrugged.

As Harley bent to cut the top wire, the man grabbed him by his shirt. I began to walk fast. Harley struggled loose and the man grabbed him again. Quicker than I could believe, Harley turned and swung at him with the hammerlike end of the cutters. I began to run. A calf kicked at me, its outstretched hoof grazing my hip. I bumped into an old cow, who jumped out of my way, then turned to swipe at me with her wandering horns. I ducked behind another animal, watching as the man pushed Harley, who toppled over backward, snagging his shirt on the barbed wire as he went down.

I stepped between them. "Enough's enough!" I said, backing him off by slapping both his shoulders with my open hands. I heard Harley swearing behind me as I stepped ahead, and suddenly the girl in Canada was slapping me on the cheek and saying, "Seventy-three points, Scooter! You're in the money!" It seemed funny to me, and I giggled to myself. She'd never called me Scooter before. But there she was, leaning over me, slapping my face and talking. Cattle milled around us, and I watched them move behind her for a while, before I let go.

"Boy," Annie said, helping me to sit up, "did he ever sucker-punch you." I gazed around. The wire was down in half a dozen places, cattle stood belly deep in the muddy water, their tails swinging as they drank.

"What happened?"

"You remember pushing the guy away from Harley?"

I nodded, trying to remember.

"Well, when you looked back to see if the old fella was all

right, the guy clipped you right in the chops. Then you took a little nap."

"Where is he?"

"They're leaving. Come on, try to stand up."

I rolled onto my knees, got one leg under myself, and stood. The pickup was across the pond, on the county road; the man with the Resistal drove, looking straight ahead. "After you went down," Annie said, steadying me with one arm around my waist, "Harley went back to his truck and laid that old cannon of his across the hood. That got their attention."

I took a step. The hills danced in a heat haze, the land loped before my eyes.

"What the hell are you grinning at? Come on, Scooter, snap out of it!" Annie pulled me along with her, and I was surprised how strong and steady she seemed on the roller-coaster ground.

Harley sat on the tailgate of his pickup, the .30-40 Krag resting on his knees. He seemed very old again, but when he looked at me, he made a fist and grinned. Lonnie glanced at me and looked away as if embarrassed. Ted took hold of my belt and led me to the shady side of the truck. He sat down with me and held up a canteen. I took a few gulps of the warm water.

"That came real close to getting western," Ted said quietly, his blue eyes fixed on mine. "I thought sure your grand-dad was going to chamber a round."

"I don't remember cutting the fence," I said.

"You didn't. Lonnie and I did."

"And Harley didn't shoot anybody?"

Ted shook his head and smiled.

"I don't feel too good," I said, just moments before realizing I was going to vomit.

14

Harley had been picking up the past few days, rising earlier, eating better, and endlessly driving the back roads, keeping track of what we were doing. He'd been burning a tank of gas a day and having a good time, yet each afternoon, during the hot part of the day, he seemed to vanish for a couple of hours. Annie and I finally caught on, when, the day after Smoke's accident, we found his truck parked in the shade of some yellow pine and Harley sound asleep in the aluminum lawn chair he carried along in back.

Harley and Smoke had an odd and old arrangement, one they had worked out before I could remember. Smoke made most of the day-to-day decisions, yet Harley was always the man in charge. As we regrouped after the scuffle, we turned to face him. He watched as the last of the cattle came back through the holes in the new fence; without looking at me, he said, "What do you think, Jack?"

I looked at the sun, still a couple hours above the snag-littered summit of Skihi peak. "We could cut Ted's, and they can start for home. Then we could take Amy's, Lonnie's, and your animals on home. Either that or start all over again tomorrow."

Harley faced me, his sharp gray eyes defined by the sweep of his hawk nose and the gullies carving his handsome old face.

"I'm all right," I said before he asked.

Harley turned to the others. "We'll cut yours first, Teddy.

77

Jackson, you work inside with Annie so we can see what you're doing with that expensive ride."

Annie and I waited until the others had circled the bunch, then rode in among the cattle and began the slow cutting of Ted's T-Lazy-T Angus. In close, Annie made every move count. A slick rider, she knew how to make cutting look easy while saving her horse. Annie's mare was a little mean, and surefooted as a cat. Together they made quite a pair.

I let her pick them, then together we pushed the animals out to the waiting riders. We tried to work it the same way each time, and pretty soon my roan was absorbed in the work. Dust slowly rose and hung in the still October air. The big herd thinned down by twos and threes, and I began to feel light-headed with the fun of it: the constant movement of the milling cattle, the catcalls from the mostly idle herders, Annie's good moves, and the quick intelligence of my roan.

If a calf tried to double back to the main bunch, the roan swung right with him, taking a couple quick steps, planting, and swinging as the calf began to turn again. And when the calf finally saw the animals beyond the riders, I'd sometimes give the roan his head and hang on as we thundered up behind him.

Finally Ted rode in too and checked the gray-backed cattle. We cut out several more, checked one last time, and rested as Ted and his sons started their cows across the slough above the pond. Harley walked out to us with his stick. "You boys just relax and let them get over Cutler Hill. Then start on our stuff. I'll be back to help you take them in."

Annie had tied her heavy hair back into two thick ponytails, which by now were stiff with dust. Trickles of sweat cut through the grit on her cheeks like tears. "Truth to tell, Harley," she said, "one of us ain't a fuckin' boy."

Harley looked her over, chewed his lip a moment, and said with a twinkle in his eye, "Never know it by the way they talk, now would you?"

We waited until Ted and his sons were out of sight after Harley drove off, then cut the last of Tanners' strays. Lonnie passed around his canteen; we drank, and wet bandannas to cool our burning faces. "Oh, for a tall, *tall* gin and tonic," Annie whispered, her bandanna folded across her eyes.

Lonnie pulled a pair of linesman pliers from a small holster on his saddle, climbed down, and handed me his reins. "I guess this won't be the last we'll see of those pugs," he said. "From now on it's going to get worse."

"It's true, you know, Scooter. We're losing more than just summer pasture." Annie draped the wet handkerchief around her neck, handed me her lines, and followed Lonnie to help him join the downed wires. She limped a little, stiff from the long days in her saddle. As I watched her walk, I told myself no: I would help them, but I could not become involved; I could stay on awhile longer, but I would not let myself care.

We headed the cattle for home, bogtrotting them across the sour slough and up the manure-speckled lane. As we rode, we let out the ends of our lariats and swung now and then at stragglers. I knew I'd have to make another phone call and was trying to find the right words to explain another delay, when I saw a mounted figure watching us from the ridge to our left. Dressed like an old-time cowboy in a historical painting, he wore a bleached-white canvas duster that covered his legs to the knee and a wide felt hat that hid the top of his face in shadow. He sat there, his hands one atop the other upon the horn, watching as we trailed the exhausted cattle toward him. He could have been a ghost, lost in time upon the prairie, watching what he could no longer expect to experience. A charge like electric shock ran through me; the hair rose on my arms. The apparition was riding my father's horse.

He waited until we reached the spot where Smoke and I had watched the coyote our first morning out, then rode in to help turn the herd east, toward the gallus frame on the abandoned Veracruz mine. Some of the older cows knew where they were going, and, remembering the sweet alsike clover and timothy of the meadows, they broke into a stiff-legged, head-swinging, downhill trot.

I dropped back to pick up a lame cow. Following her, I watched the others ride on ahead. Across the mass of moving heads and haunches, I could see Lonnie and Annie flanking the jogging stock. Harley rode behind, the Walker stepping out in his long, rolling stride, his head high and alert. The riders and cattle moved ahead of me through the blue sage and swaying native grasses, burning now in the rich last light of the day. On the flat above the Veracruz, my grandfather turned them toward the single pine that marked the beginning of the wing fence, just as he had done dozens of times before I was born. The cattle began to lope as they neared the timber, pressing together and running, some twisting and bucking for the clumsy fun of it as they gained speed. The horsemen fanned out behind, and together they disappeared into the trees, vanishing in the late afternoon light, one last time, into the hidden, waiting wings of the blind corral.

15

This is going to smart," I said, as Harley turned his back to me. He'd stripped to a T-shirt made from a winter long-underwear top. His exposed, blue-white upper arms were thin, his bony shoulders frail. I took his thin arm, and, as gently as I could, swabbed a cottonball saturated with iodine down the ugly barbed-wire cut running from shoulder to elbow. He flinched and swore at the bite of antiseptic.

Although the stringy muscle of his arm was as hard and twisted as a pitch root, I couldn't imagine how he'd managed to lift Smoke's heavy stock saddle onto the Walker. I watched as he struggled into a chambray shirt and remembered him swinging on the man at the water hole with his fencing tool. If he'd been my age, I suspected, things would have turned out very differently for the man in the brown Resistal.

But he was not my age, and the excitement and strain of the past days seemed to have taken more out of him than he was prepared to give. He was tired in a way that rest did not seem to cure; ill, perhaps, beyond any sickness I could imagine. And in spite of myself, I found excuses for getting away. "I'm going to work out, Harley. Need anything before I go upstairs?"

"Just some peace and quiet," he answered, pouring himself a tall glass of milk. "So don't be banging those weights on the floor up there all night."

I had worked out a schedule, starting with a jog around

the meadows and twenty minutes of stretching out, then sit-ups on an inclined board, push-ups, and four sets of six different lifts. I usually finished by doing pull-ups on two looped strands of five-eighths logging cable hanging from the squared ceiling beams. The workouts helped me through the evenings, burning up the chilly hours after sunset when Harley watched television or dozed in his recliner. They gave me something to measure myself by and time to think. I imagined myself getting stronger, and as I lifted, I chanted Summer's cantos of pain, dreaming of riding well, of winning once again. My brother had always been working on his strength and moves, and he'd pulled me along, tricking me into working harder than I would have on my own, pushing me further than I could ever have gone alone. Now that I had only myself, I never missed a night, and no matter how tired, I did a little more each evening. When I tired to the point of quitting, I read again the card on the wall above Summer's side of the desk: "If there's not at least a little hurt in your life every day, you're not living hard enough."*

Beside the telephone I kept a notepad, where each morning I jotted down my responsibilities for the coming day. I'd crossed out each item except two: *Call Smoke. Call Canada.* I wrapped a gym towel around my sweating neck and dialed the hospital.

"Heckethorn," Smoke answered.

"How's the leg?" I asked, holding the receiver in my left hand and doing one-handed curls with my right. "Ready to go after your elk yet?"

Smoke mumbled something away from the receiver. I heard a woman laugh. "Saw the x rays today—nice clean break, right beside some old ones."

"You ought to be able to predict the weather clear to Idaho now, old man."

He laughed, and we blue-skied for a few minutes. When I

*Courtesy of Paul Zarzyski.

asked, Smoke offered some advice on the various ways of sorting cattle in the maze of chutes at the corrals. He sounded in good spirits, and as we said our good-byes, I heard the lady laugh again.

Half sweat, half analgesic liniment, my room had begun to smell like a locker room, even with the dormer windows open. I did two sets of push-ups and six sets of presses, grunting out a few extra of each, putting off the last item on the list as long as I could. When I'd hit the road to rodeo, the world had been a plum to be picked; Smoke and Summer and Harley took care of themselves without much help from anyone. Now, it seemed, I'd found the worms in the fruit. Being necessary made me uneasy; although I was older, the urge to be gone had grown even stronger.

Her mother answered the phone. A statuesque woman who looked like an older sister, she was always cheerful and polite. But there was a distance between us that hadn't narrowed since we'd first met, a distance or distrust, perhaps, only strengthened after Summer went down in the Highlands and I'd left the next day on the bus. "She's right here, Jack," her mother said, and I listened to distance hum on the line.

"Hey, partner, I just walked down to the arena and back without crutches."

A drop of sweat fell from my forehead to the bare wooden table, spreading in a dark stain as it disappeared into the dry wood. I wondered if it was her voice that held me, if I was in love with a sound.

"Just one cane," she said, "and it won't be long before I won't need that. You'll be surprised how straight I can walk when you come. No more gimping around for this girl."

"You and my old man ought to get together. He just broke a leg." I explained about Smoke's wreck and Harley's condition as well as I could. "I'm sorry," I told her, "but there's nobody else they can count on right now, and I just can't leave them the way they are."

"You're going to stay then?"

"Just until things straighten out. Won't make the immigration hearing on time, but I can't see any way around that."

"Jack?"

"Come on now, pal—"

"Don't you— would you rather—" Her quiet voice trailed off, becoming secretive or shy. I tried to conjure her face and failed.

"But listen. I've been riding every day, and I've started working out. When I get up there I'll be like new."

She laughed. "Do you want me to call immigration?"

"Yes, would you? Let's try for a new date, maybe in early November after things settle out here. What about this man Kittredge?"

"He's a hell of a hand, Jack, the real deal. But he'll need someone out to his place soon. I'll check on that too."

The line hummed, the yellow pines beyond my window rustled in the evening breeze, and her face came to me in the dark. "I still miss you," I said to the image in the night air.

"Cowboys never miss anyone for long," she said. "Not in this life."

The last animal cleared the back of the truck; the driver let his rope go, and dry pulleys screeched as the tailgate whistled closed. "That's it!" Ted waved and climbed over the manure-slick chute with the shipping papers in one hand.

I walked back down a plank alleyway, closing gates and watching Harley through cracks between the boards. He stood alone in the big corral, surrounded by Amy's milling holdovers, watching the last load of his cattle jostle the forty-foot semi. I closed the holding-pen gate and flicked the hondo end of my rope at a passing heifer. My jeans were spattered with cow shit; both my shins were black and blue where the wild spring calves had managed to kick me. Although I liked cattle, after two days of sorting, clipping, branding, and loading, I'd had enough of them to last me awhile.

Honest Barry Kitterman tucked his checkbook into a western-cut jacket and stepped into his Continental, then waved and pulled away, throwing gravel. The truck driver kicked chocks from under his rear wheels and climbed into the cab of the Peterbilt. The truck groaned up the long hill toward the house; we watched, not looking at each other, until it was out of sight.

Harley pulled his clipboard from a nail on the loading chute, turned pages, and tallied by fives on a plank with a blunt pencil. He counted again the list of ear-tag numbers we'd identified against those on the sheets. "Looks like we're short about nineteen cows, eight two-year-old heifers, four big steers, one old bull, maybe a dozen calves. Pretty good chunk of money, even on today's market."

He unwrapped a stick of gum and folded it twice before putting it in his mouth. "Tell you what," he said, chewing carefully with his remaining teeth. "Jackson, you find 'em and bring them in. I'll give you a bill of sale for any you catch. You can sell 'em for your wages or put them on pasture here. You want to keep them, I'll throw in the F L Bar, too."

Annie and Ted laughed about something as they boxed their gear on the catwalk above the loading chute. I didn't say anything.

"You're going to stick around awhile, aren't you?"

"Well, until Smoke can walk, sure."

"Now you're coming to. All that noise about Canada can wait. You don't have to catch 'em all at once. Take your time. Catch a few when you want. You've got a month of dry ground yet. Maybe you can get Annie to give you a hand."

I glanced at Harley, but he looked back with a straight face. The roan, I noticed, was dozing beside the log barn.

He'd brought me a long way back already, becoming, during the past few weeks, a twelve-hundred-pound buddy. I'd have to stay, there was no way around it, and with the roan I might make wages—like Harley said, work when I wanted. "Why not?" I answered. "You've got a deal." Why not, I thought as we shook on it. After all, I had nothing to lose but time.

16

Annie rode her mare side to side behind her mother's cattle until the last one was in the lane. I closed the pole gate, caught up with her, and we lazed along, letting the cattle graze as we left the timber. "How's Smokey feeling?" she asked, lifting her Denver Broncos baseball cap to brush back some wild red hairs.

"The leg was broken in two places, but he says they look clean in the x-rays. To tell the truth, I think he's almost happy to have a rest."

Annie stuffed her gloves into the gullet of her saddle. "And how's Harley taking all this?"

"I'm not privy to most of the conversations he has with himself, although sometimes I can hear him a hundred yards off, arguing his case with someone I can't see."

Annie smiled. I lit a smoke, wet the match between my thumb and finger, and put it in my pocket. "I've seen him better, though. That's for sure."

"Momma's not much good either. Her hands just kill her at night."

"What are you going to do about this pasture deal?"

"I don't know. Mom's got the lawyer coming out this morning over something else. We might end up leasing pasture next year, which will mean trucking twice and more outlay." Annie shook her head and bummed my cigarette. "All at once it seems so much is happening out here. I'm beginning to feel like a trespasser on ground we've taken for granted all our lives."

Annie had gained a little weight over the years. No longer girlish or willowy, she filled her bib overalls in just the right places. I enjoyed watching her as she talked, her brown eyes friendly, her weathered face fine, and I realized that she was good-looking in a way you don't see much anymore, kind of rough, honest-homely, and pretty all wrapped together.

"What's this lady friend of yours think about you hanging around down here?"

"I talked with her last night. It's not what we'd planned, but I think she understands. She's pretty tough-minded. Got hurt in a barrel race, you know, when I was in Oklahoma. Pulled a hip apart that had already been cut on twice. Now she's walking on canes and talking quarter horses again. She'll stick."

Annie pulled her mare over against my roan, put her arm around me, and kissed me on the cheek. "You're all right, Scooter," she said and tipped my hat down over my eyes.

We had a late start; the warm October morning and the grazing cows plodding up ahead made my eyes heavy. The grass-hungry cattle took a step, pulled a bite of the cured grass, switched their silky tails at lazy flies, and took another step. We eased them through the wire gate beside the cattle guard, where Harley's homemade road entered his place, then let them graze down Cutler Hill.

Annie reached over and touched my face. "That bother you much?"

"Only when I laugh, good-looking."

"Don't bullshit a bullshitter."

"Sure it bothers me some. Good thing I had my mouth shut though."

"Hum?"

"Doctors said I'd have lost my tongue if my teeth hadn't stopped the iron. This other"— I lifted my hat and touched the white hair above my ear—"well, that was worse than it looks."

"Jumping Jesus, Scooter, what happened?"

"Short round. Loaded one up with a bum fuse. Went off about fifty feet from the end of the tube. I don't think about it much now."

Annie watched me, didn't say anything, except to grunt for another drag on my smoke.

I pointed my chin at the cattle. "So why didn't Amy work something out with Harley on leaving these old sisters at his place? He's got pasture galore."

"You know how Momma is about Harley."

"Well, sure, but . . ."

"She's always got to be so tough."

"She *is* pretty tough, if you ask me."

"Scooter, she hurts all the time."

We crossed the county road, turned above the dredge pond, crossed the slough, and kept the cattle moving up the grassy flat, away from the brush in Rocker Gulch. Survey ribbons hung in the scrubby trees to our right. A contrail crossed the sky to the west. I was looking for the plane when Annie said, "Listen!" and stopped her mare. High in the boulder-studded hills that flanked Skihi peak, I heard distant barking.

"They're running deer again," Annie said.

"Wild dogs?"

"Nope. They come up Tucker Gulch from those new places this side of Unionville. Smoke said they're all over Harley's south end, from the developments across the highway."

"Funny, I haven't seen any."

"You will. Blow them away when you do."

"I don't know."

"You listen to me, Scooter. I've killed four since haying. They were all in packs and they all had collars. They chase around all day, then go home for dinner. They're well fed, but they'll be after our calves next, and no telling what else, if we give them the slack."

The aspen gulches ran like bright paint up the mountain.

Granite monuments of enormous, weather-rounded boulders stood upright and stark along the tops of the ridges. I scanned the skyline, remembering how once, while Harley and Smoke and I had been digging a cattle guard at Amy's, we'd seen a huge, tannish bear in the rocks up there, rolling logs for ants. We'd watched him with Harley's binoculars for a good ten minutes, convinced, despite the distance, that he was a grizzly.

We turned the cows into a small hay field at Amy's. They fanned out, picking delicately at tender alfalfa shoots stooling from the mown stubble. They ignored us, knowing they were home. "If you'll take care of these hay burners, I'll buy the beer," Annie offered, stepping down from her dappled mare.

I led our horses into the shaded corral under the old firs behind Amy's barns, pulled the saddles and bridles, and turned Annie's mare out with the cattle. I sat on a rock and rolled the last of my Dominion tobacco. The roan turned over on his back in the dust, lazy, and satisfied that we'd done a full day. The autumn light, filtering through the trees, or perhaps the mild tobacco, brought an unexpected sense of the October days she and I had shared in Canada. I sat and smoked, satisfied too, remembering the drives between those late indoor shows. I hadn't been used to winning, like some of the riders I'd seen every weekend all season. But she'd helped me with that too, making it seem a natural end to hard work and concentration.

When Annie didn't reappear, I wandered down to the back porch, took a beer from the propane refrigerator, and hung my hat on the lowest tine of a moth-eaten shoulder-mounted buck on the wall beside the door. I found Annie and her mother sitting at the table in the sunny dining room, looking out at the grazing cattle.

"I don't believe it. Not for a second," Amy said. "It should have been on the abstract and isn't. It's just dirt."

"What's the lawyer say?" Annie asked, staring at her mother.

"He thinks it looks like they have a case, that they actually did get a title on unpaid back taxes."

"But how did they find out? Why didn't we ever get wind of it?"

"I don't know, girl. But I can tell you this. While we're working, trying to keep our place up, they've got a couple henchmen trying to figure a way of getting it for nothing." Amy struck a wooden match on the sole of her boot and lit one of her machine-rolled Bugler cigarettes. She waved her hand through the cloud of smoke. "Sit down, Jackson. Don't stand there like a post."

I hesitated. "Is this any of my business?"

"Oh, sit down," Amy answered. "Of course it is."

Annie looked at me, and for the first time I could remember—since we'd been kids, when she'd tried once too often to bully Summer and he'd popped her one—she had tears in her eyes. She stared at me for a second, got up, and went outside.

I held the icy bottle in my clasped hands. The cuckoo clock opened above my head, the little wooden bird lurched out and sang his wooden song. I raised my eyebrows, curious, but not wanting to ask.

"They say they own a twenty-acre patented hard-rock claim right here where my buildings are. Got it by paying back taxes. *Twenty acres,* including the land right under this house! They're going to take me to court for trespassing, and I've lived here since 1931. Can you believe that?"

"Who is, Amy?"

She squinted her wrinkly face in disbelief. "Well Tanners, of course." She released a blue fog from her nose and raised the cigarette with her gnarled fingers for another long drag. "You don't know anybody else around here that would pull something like that, do you?"

"No ma'am, I sure don't."

"You watch and see: They're after my whole place. They'll take me to court, win, devalue my place by cutting this chunk out of the center." She blew a smoke ring, then fired a cannonball through it. "But they are in for a surprise. They ain't going to get my whole place. If I have to, I'll jack up everything that ain't growin' and move it off their damned twenty acres and put a locked gate out front!"

"I don't see why there's this sudden interest in this old dry land," I said, killing the beer. "What's the point?"

"Money's the point. Town is growing, Boy. It's moving toward us, and we're right smack in the way."

I peeled the label from the bottle, wanting another and remembering a summer night at a drive-in I'd spent drinking beer with Summerfield and his rodeo buddies, watching *The Blob*. We'd thought it was pretty funny and took to yelling along with the fleeing families on the screen, "The BLOB is coming! The BLOB is coming!" until the college-kid manager told us to leave.

"Jackson?" Amy said, lowering her voice. "That grandfather of yours got a good will?"

"Hell, I don't know."

"You find out. Make damn sure he does. Otherwise that place of his becomes an estate, and those jackals will fall on you and Smoke like dogs on sheep." She tucked her bony chin and lowered her voice still more. "I'll tell you something else. You keep an eye on that little chippy Smoke's running with too. Believe me, she's out for more than just a good time."

17

I hid the roan in a stand of wind-turned fir and clambered up a talus slide to the rocky crest of Harris Hill. When I'd caught my breath, I hung Harley's binoculars around my neck, pulled on my gloves, and hand-over-handed my way up the brittle limbs of a half-dead limber pine. I leaned against the gnarled trunk and looked at the sweep of country below, at the hazed hills in the distance and the flats beneath me, still bordered by the back furrows of Tom Flavven's gang plows. Beyond his house, the tiny pond he and Harley had built with teams and an iron-wheeled fresno shimmered in the midmorning light.

Through the glasses, in startling detail, I could see tire tracks cresting each white-rocked knob on the Harris place, the distinct features of every gray-stoned gulch, and, lying in the brushy draws, an occasional red splotch of a bedded animal half hidden in knee-deep grass. Although Tanners' hired help had spent a week moving their stock to portable corrals beyond the old Hirsch place, they, like us, had missed a few. The remaining cattle had scattered into ones and twos after being disrupted. Cows and spring calves hung together, but everything else seemed content to wander alone.

Finding Harley's strays in all that country was a little like hunting elk. I used the binoculars and then the roan, trying to locate and later catch them in open country.

I shifted the glasses north, checking each low hill beyond

the county road. Beyond the Keltch place I heard a rifle shot, then another. I moved the glasses an inch at a time, until I noticed a movement in some scattered trees. I held my breath, focused the lens, and saw two riders contouring through the timber. They rode out of sight behind a ridge, heading in the direction of the Hirsch place, half a mile beyond the new quarry.

Since the scuffle at the water hole, I'd kept my eyes open, avoiding the white pickups and horse trailers and riders who seemed to be everywhere at once. More than anything, the time they wasted riding the now waterless land to the west showed their lack of understanding of a country they claimed to own. They were many, and I was one; they made lots of dust and plenty of noise. Yet without further contact, I took Harley's cattle home and turned them loose in his meadows. Those stragglers were the first cattle I had ever owned, and as they grazed in the evenings among the aspen, they grew sleek in my eyes.

Harley stepped onto the porch where I'd taken to smoking after supper. He latched the door and tugged on the visor of his railroad cap: a relief pitcher about to enter the last home game. "Let's go for a drive, Pilgrim," he said, eyeing the cattle too. "Seeing as how you're supposed to be working for me, I figure to get some work out of you. Wood room's empty. Come on, I'll show you a few snags you can buck up."

We headed for the south end of the place, where Harley's father had homesteaded first. I drove slow, stopping now and then to look at the dead trees Harley pointed out. They stood alone, above timber of a later growth, their brittle limbs scraping an empty sky.

We followed cow trails in and out of the timber, through parks and hay fields, occasionally seeing the white rumps of mule deer bouncing off through the scattered bull pine. We crisscrossed his neglected hay fields, overgrown now with Ranger alfalfa and a variety of wheat grasses. Until Summerfield and I had been in grade school, Harley had grain-farmed this land. Even if we had been too young to be much help, we'd picked rock and harrowed a lot of weekends that our little buddies spent at the Y shooting baskets.

Dry-land farming, celebrated now only by rusting tin signs nailed to decaying sheds: "This farm uses the Ferguson System." Each fall, turn the land under, two furrows at a time, and in the spring, disk the earth to death; pick rock for days, then harrow it across the grain, breathing the fine dust that worked deep into bearings and teeth, distributors and lungs, wiring and eyes. How many times had I seen my father working on the stalled Fordson tractor, in wind that cut through any cloth made, his hands black and his face dark with rage?

I didn't see how plowing and planting could have been done with horses on such a scale in such rough country. But for much of three men's lives it had been done; the horses dragged the implements until the iron wore out, and places were named where favorites had died in harness. A rock pile for Old Frank, a dry wash for Conn, a stand of pine later, for Conn's mate, Kelly. Places honored by naming, hallowed by the memory of what it was to die pulling a plow.

For the last fifteen years, Harley had cultivated alfalfa hay, and each year now it came of itself. Each spring we towed a drag of railroad iron and tractor tires around the fields to spread mole hills, level gopher mounds, and break up manure. We pulled it with a pickup, and in a good day a man could cover forty acres, out of the wind and dust, listening to the radio or reading a paperback.

We topped a rocky point and saw a three-quarter-ton truck parked beside the boundary fence. A lone man worked the ratchet handle on a wire stretcher. He straightened when he heard us, then bent again to join the rusty strands. I pulled opposite his outfit and killed the engine.

"What say, Easy Money?" Ted Schillings asked, his blue eyes bright as neon in his ruddy, wind-burned face. Not a big man, he got as much done in a day as anyone. The years of labor showed, though, in the slope of his shoulders, the curve of his bent back. Yet he worked on alone, even into the dusk, doing what he knew ought to be done.

Harley and I got out and faced him across the fence. Ted's father and Harley had been enemies. Although we got along fine, there was that clouded past, a sense of clans that never went completely away, a distance we didn't try to narrow.

"Those survey crews just go where they want." Ted gestured with his cutters at the end of a rusted wire. The tip showed the bright bite of pliers.

Harley took the wire in his hand and looked at it with mild interest. "Wonder what they're up to now?" he asked.

"Must have needed to back-shoot a reference point from somewhere in your place, Harley. They've been hanging ribbon from the Kennedy Flat to the head of Jackson this week. Looks like a used-car lot above my meadows."

Harley looked off toward Sheep Mountain, then back to Ted. "Won't be long, they'll have us surrounded."

Ted put his tools in the clutter of cedar posts and wire, saws and shovels, axes and hammers heaped in his truck. He brought a yellow folder from the cab and, with his finger, drew a circle on a blueprintlike map. "Five-acre lots," he said. "All of Rocker and Casey Creek clear to the highway. They been down to see you yet?"

"Not lately," Harley answered. "And I don't expect to see them either. You heard what they're pulling on Amy?"

Ted nodded and placed the map back in the folder. "They write big checks that don't bounce," he said, his thoughts flickering across his face. He noticed the wire stretcher hanging where he'd left it when we'd driven up. "Bigger checks than a dozen lifetimes on my place could cover."

"I want to show you something. Pull up over there." Harley pointed toward a fenced enclosure where we had stacked rye hay when he first bought a baler. We had used army-surplus hospital tents to cover the stacks, and ragged chunks of rotten canvas still flapped on the barbed wire fence.

"See that snag?" Harley aimed his finger at a burled, limbless log wedged between two boulders. "My dad and I cut that. Bottom was full of ants was why we didn't take it all." He looked at the ax marks that still showed where limbs had been lopped off, then closed his eyes. "We stopped for a smoke that morning," he said. "Sat down on a rock for a few minutes over there to rest. Well, sir, one of those big black carpenter ants had crawled up the inside of my coveralls," Harley's eyes snapped open, "and he bit me right on the head of my pecker!"

Harley laughed a laugh too deep to come from his sunken chest. I chuckled too, seeing him in my imagination, coming off the rock, his kid's eyes wild. "Ran halfway to the creek before I got my pants down. Hollered most of the way— made such a sudden racket, me yelling and my dad laughing, that we spooked the team. They busted loose and took off for the barn. When I sulled back up here, with my bottom lip stuck out, the old man took one look at me and started in all over again. Laughed himself right down to his hands and knees." Tears ran down my grandfather's cheeks from laughing. "God, but I missed that man," he said. "After he did himself in."

Harley began to cough. He struggled for breath, got it, and coughed again. When the spasms passed, he wiped his eyes. "That was one of the few times I recall him ever letting go. He was usually such a hard case—reminded me a lot of your dad."

He cleared his throat, chuckled, and said, "Leave that one go. There's plenty of dead wood around." He seemed to consider something for a minute, then climbed from the truck and waved for me to follow. Partly hidden by the butt of the old snag and completely surrounded by clumps of buckbrush stood a flat stone with an X chiseled across its surface. Harley knelt before it and drew his fingers along the chipped, intersecting lines. "This is what they were looking for, the surveyors. The section corner that centers this end of the place." He touched the stone again as if it were a holy relic and added, "You might need to know where it is some-day, Pilgrim."

III

18

Annie waited outside while I tried to help Smoke get dressed. I felt like we were springing an inmate from Alcatraz, and Smoke—banging around the room in his cast like a cub bear with one foot in a lard bucket—didn't make the job any easier. I tried to calm him down by talking.

"Two of Tanners' people stopped to see Harley this morning," I said, trying to get his pants leg over the plaster cast. "Harley was nice as pie, had them in for coffee, acted like they'd been neighbors for twenty years." The pants were too tight; I pulled them back off.

"Yeah?" Smoke said, buttoning his shirt, one button off, from top to bottom. "He can do that. But I'll tell you what Tanners are going to run into with him." He paused, noticed the extra button, and started again. "One time, when I was just a kid, Harley made a deal with the governor in Helena on a load of stove wood. Two dollars, delivered. Times were tough, one place after another was being abandoned around us, we were living on macaroni and deer meat."

I cut the inseam of his pants to above the knee with the bone-handled Case knife I found in his pocket. Smoke began buttoning the shirt again, staring at the wall above me, trying to remember the story.

"So. Harley brought in a load of dead wood in lengths, bucksawed every stick by hand, split it, ricked it in his lumber wagon, and hauled it the eight miles to town with a team. At the governor's mansion he had to carry it an armload at a time up some stairs, through a kitchen, and down a winding staircase to the cellar, where he stacked it all nice and neat."

The split leg fit over the cast. I pulled the pants down enough to get the other leg started, then got out of the way as he thrashed into them.

"When he'd brought in the whole load, he had to wait an hour or so before the governor got around to seeing him. By then Harley'd spent that two bucks ten times in his head." Smoke rocked away from the bed and zipped his pants.

"Well, the governor goes down to the basement and looks at the wood. Then he comes upstairs and tells Harley he'll pay him a buck and a half for the load. Harley reminds him the deal was two dollars for a wagonload of split wood. The governor says it's only worth a buck fifty. Take it or leave it."

I stuffed the robe, pajamas, and slippers I'd bought for him the week before into a paper sack. "Right," I said, not paying much attention.

Smoke touched my arm. "Harley says, all right, *fine*. And he carries every stick back up those stairs, through the kitchen, down the outside steps, and stacks it in the wagon again. We were all counting on those groceries, you know, but when Harley got home there weren't any groceries. It was pitch dark when I helped him unhook the horses. And it was macaroni and venison for supper again that night."

Smoke pulled a sock onto his good foot. "That governor was a Republican. Harley's voted in every election since, and right or wrong, he's voted Democrat every time. If LBJ had run again, Harley might have voted against him. But he never forgave the Republican Party for that load of wood, and he's not going to forget about these new people closing the range either."

Annie rapped on the door. A moment later a nurse the size of a Russian weight lifter padded into the room. She stared at Smoke and put her hands on her massive hips. "Are you planning to go somewhere, dear?"

"I'm going home and lay on my butt and save the hundred bucks a day you're fleecing me for this room."

She looked doubtful. "I'll have to check on this. You should have told someone. Just wait until I come back, won't you, dear?" She lumbered away, the door closing behind her with a soft hiss.

"Can I help you, dear?" I asked Smoke as he hopped across the room, trying to untangle his suspenders. He growled and grinned and got them straightened by himself.

"I got the helicopter people on the phone this morning," I said. "You know what they told me? 'Call our attorney.'"

"I won't need to go through their lawyer."

"Don't even think about it, Smoke."

"Hand me my boots—boot, will you?"

I held out the oiled White's Packer. When he took hold, I hung on. "Summer flew them too, the choppers."

Smoke stepped into the boot and laced it without looking up. He stood, put one hand on my shoulder for balance, and said, "I hadn't thought of it like that."

The door swung open and Sandy Martinez walked in, her designer jeans latex-tight on her slender legs. She kissed the old man and he goosed her. She giggled and struggled in his powerful arms, seeming glad to be caught. I stood with Smoke's extra boot in my hand until Annie opened the door for the nurse, who entered pushing a wheelchair.

"Just hop in and I'll take you down to Admissions, dear," she said, jolly as a bear again.

"I can make it with these," Smoke answered, starting for the door on the worn pair of crutches I'd retrieved from his tack room.

"Insurance regulations, Mr. Heckethorn."

"I'll catch a ride with Sandy here, if you kids want to take off. Right, Babe?"

"Sure," Sandy said, looking at me. Her grapeshot-gray eyes lingered on the white streak in my hair. "You kids can take off," she echoed, "or not."

Smoke took another hop on his crutches and the nurse

shouldered her way toward the door, confronting him with her enormous breasts. "Mr. Heckethorn, please!"

"Mr. Heckethorn was my granddaddy, dear," Smoke said, and stepped around her into the hall. She looked at me for help. I shrugged. Behind her, we could hear the rubber tips of the crutches squeaking down the waxed corridor, squeaking like rubber-soled shoes on the waxed floors of nightmare land. I handed Sandy Martinez Smoke's spare boot.

Annie moved her lips as she read the menu at the Country Kitchen. She looked younger, dressed in a lacy long-sleeved blouse and camel-colored skirt. Her hair, tied back, folded gently around each cheek. My eyes lingered on her full breasts.

"Scooter!" Annie said and lifted the menu to her cleft chin.

"Sorry," I said and looked through the glass beside our booth at the frantic traffic on Prospect Avenue.

"You sure are," she said. "You know, you probably ought to get to town more often. You've spent all your time either working or with Harley since you've been back in this country. That's not healthy, it's really not."

The waitress came and took our orders. She took the menus too. I stared out the window, at the pizza parlors, drive-in banks, insurance offices and real-estate companies lining the busy street. I could remember coming to town one time with Harley when I was a boy. Prospect Avenue had been a rutted dirt road through shacks and empty prairie. We had hauled, I remembered, rough lumber from a sawmill not a block from where we now sat. "What would you do, if you were me?" I asked.

"About what? Getting laid?"

I had trouble meeting her eyes. "About Harley and Smoke. It seems everything I've touched has turned wrong since I've been back."

"You've made a real difference for all of us. Don't be a jerk."

"Smoke says he'll have to move Harley down to the valley after I leave."

"He'd better take some blasting caps and powder if he's going to move Harley anywhere."

"That's right, isn't it?" I felt a sad tingle of pride in my face.

"I imagine Smokey's going to have his hands full just taking care of himself on those crutches."

I nodded, my gaze returning to the buttons on Annie's blouse. What rose in me, I finally recognized as desire. When I glanced up, Annie looked me full in the face, reached across the table, and put her warm hand on mine. "You've done good, honey," she said softly. "But maybe you better head on north pretty soon, before you get lost. If you wait on Harley and Smoke, you'll get left holding a bag."

"Like the night you and Summer took me to the reservoir hunting snipe?"

"Just like that, only nobody's going to come back with a flashlight when the fun's over."

I turned my hand palm up and held her fingers. "I'm going to wait awhile. That's all I can do. Meanwhile, we're still missing about ten head of stock. Harley wants me to beat the brush for them."

"Well, let me know if you want some company. Long as you promise not to stare at my milkers all the time."

I could feel the blood in my face, the throb in my groin. I took my hand away.

"You know," Annie confided, "that little twitch has been good for your dad. He was such a mess after Summer got killed. All the time work, work, work. He wasn't eating right, stayed off by himself, and he'd blow up at the drop of a hat. Then you got hurt and didn't come home. He got worse. Had a couple of bad fights uptown. Almost went to jail over one."

Annie's eyes crinkled at the corners. "Then they got together. It was a big secret at first, but pretty soon I was running into them all over town, Smokey with a big grin and his old grab-it-and-growl confidence back."

"Maybe that's what I need," I said.

"You should see them dance," Annie went on. "The Country Swing moves they've got worked out! Smoke so happy, Sandy high as the moon."

19

I followed the smell, and when I finally found her, I rode upwind. The carcass was scattered in a patch of waist-high wild rose where she must have lain down to shelter against a storm. Parts of her had been dragged away by coyotes or dogs, but the bulk of her body remained intact, held together by her rotting hide. Ribs and vertebrae, exposed by the pecking of birds, had already begun to bleach. I stepped down and coaxed the white-eyed roan up closer so I could look for identifying marks.

Her head lay several yards downhill, earless and balding under the autumn sun. I searched the ground in widening circles for the plastic ear tag but found nothing. I clamped my nose and bent to look for a brand. And I saw—under the leathery waste of her haunch, beneath what remained of her tail—the delicate, protruding forelegs of the calf that had killed her, arched toward life.

Most evenings I began my workouts by jogging a mile or so along the deer trails weaving through the rocky bluffs between Harley's and Ford's. I wasn't serious about the running, but it was a good way to warm up, get loose, and rediscover, at the same time, places I'd all but forgotten.

One evening, on my way back from Ford's, I crossed the creek below the log barn and trotted through a dark stand of giant firs growing along the south bank. It was damp among the old trees; late mushrooms grew on fallen logs and on the moss-carpeted stumps of trees felled by French-Canadian woodcutters before the turn of the century. The still air was sweet with the rich scent of decay.

The trail wandered past a grassy park where Harley had run one of his whiskey stills. On the far side of the opening, suspended between four trees by light chains, hung the bucking barrel my brother had built to improve his riding.

Summer's friends had come often to Harley's in the evenings to take turns on the barrel. One would ride while the others lifted and pulled on the chains, causing the barrel to leap and dive. The longer you clung to the surcingle, the harder the others worked to pitch you off, and usually the harder they tried, the farther you fell.

I jiggled one of the rusted chains. Summer had put me on the barrel a lot of evenings when no one else was around, and he'd kept me on, until he couldn't throw me off by himself. One night, after he and his friends had worn themselves out, a bronc rider named Zupan asked me why I didn't climb on. I remembered how I'd tried to be cool. "No, guess not," I'd said, and scuffed the battered toe of my boot in the mossy duff.

Summer took a hit on a passing pint of Kessler's. "He can ride it, Zupe," he said and pulled his wallet. "Am I wrong, Bub?"

I saw what was coming, stuffed my hands in my pockets, and shook my head no. "Five says he can." Summer pulled a bill and held it folded between the swollen knuckles of his right hand. Zupan studied me a minute, dug in his pocket, and covered the bet.

I climbed onto the rust-thinned barrel and sat, swinging between the trees, listening to the voices of the creek, watching the shadows deepen among the firs. Summer—in the early stages of what was to become the looping Ho Chi Minh mustache that later carved his bull-trout chin—helped me wrap the braided bull rope around my gloved hand, telling me to stay astraddle that hand and keep my eyes focused just beyond the top rim of the barrel. I remembered clearly the barrel rising behind me, turning and falling. I gripped with all the strength in my legs, pulled with all the strength in my arm, and stared into that swooping space above the barrel's flying rim as it spun and dipped, rose and fell. I pulled until I felt the ligaments stretch in my riding arm, until my head swam, until the cowboys tired and gradually quit. They had held nothing back and neither had I. Summer stuffed the five he'd won in my pocket; Zupan passed the Kessler's. They were my first winnings and my first taste of whiskey: my initiation into a world of possibility called Rodeo Dreams.

I slid from the barrel and started through the trees toward the house. In the dusk, it seemed he ran before me, leading me on with his confidence, pulling me as he always had, by the sheer force of heart.

We crossed the county road below the new quarry and made for the gentle hills to the north. Annie stood in her stirrups and shaded her eyes, looking at the hillside ahead. "You been up in there yet?" she asked, looking back over her shoulder.

I shook my head and watched her ride on, smiling to myself at the graceful yet masculine way she handled herself on horseback. We picked up a cow trail and rode single file into the trees. Some places I had to lay against the roan's neck to avoid dry limbs, and, smelling the rich coffee scent of his damp hair, the sweet, burnt odor of horse, I felt suddenly very proud of us both for the way he'd finished out.

The trail contoured gradually up through thinning patches of pine and juniper, then doubled back and opened into a bowl-like swale dotted with clumps of waist-high sage. A dozen magpies, startled by our quiet approach, leaped light-boned into flight ahead.

We started across the coulee, and there, plain upon the short grass, but hidden in the sage at a distance, lay two bloated carcasses. Annie handed me her reins and stepped down. She walked through them, looking at brands, then bent to study one's head. "Oh boy, Scooter," she said, her voice going low and strange. "You'd better look at this."

I coaxed the roan past the swollen animals. Annie's mare snorted once, then pulled a bite of grass, dismissing the death around her. Annie and I hunkered together, as if praying to the maggot-moving head. Centered above the eye sockets, a small round hole the size of a marble burned into the curly white forehead hair of Harley's missing bull.

"Some shot," Annie whispered, and I heard her voice continue, as if I was under water, or a great distance away. *That boy . . . the boy at the gun . . . goes rigid, clenching the lanyard in his shaking hand. A cartoon of fear, he stares at me with wide, white eyes. I clamp my jaw and start toward him from behind the trails when the order comes, and he hesitates, as I know he will, then jerks the rope. The sky flares into yellow-white noise as the howitzer, bursting and on fire, rears skyward in a flash of hot light. Concussion, and I'm down, seeing my trainees leap and somersault like puppets beside the wounded gun. But their strings pop and they fall to earth like men. And as the bloody light begins to fail, the screams begin . . .*

"Stop it, Scooter! What's wrong with you?" Annie was shaking me by the front of my jacket, her face inches from mine. Behind her I saw my roan, dragging the lines I'd dropped. He stood munching cured grass, looking back over his shoulder at us. I tried to slow my breathing, avoiding Annie's eyes. Then I put my arms around her and watched the horse chew. Annie held me like she meant it.

"It doesn't usually catch me like that during the day," I tried to explain. "I'm sorry."

"You scared me silly. You should have seen your face." Annie rubbed my back through my denim jacket, her cheek touching mine. For a long time neither of us moved.

"Annie, let's not say anything about this for a while."

"Hey, Scooter, I won't—"

"No. I mean these animals."

Annie stepped back, swept loose hair from her eyes, and frowned. "You better get a stock inspector out here pronto and turn it in at the sheriff's office before all you have here is a pile of bones."

I looked at the deformed and random poses the cattle had assumed in death, at the empty eye sockets pecked hollow by the magpies, at the swollen tongues protruding from rigid jaws. I remembered hearing the shots from Harris Hill and seeing the riders making off through the trees.

"Annie, if I'm ever going to get out of here, I've got to avoid more trouble, not stir it up. I was only going to sell them anyway, so it doesn't really matter."

The friendship went out of Annie's eyes. "Well, fine. Fuck it," she said and turned her back on the whole idea.

The next morning I picked up their tracks just beyond the carcasses. Both horses had been shod with bar shoes, and the deep clean prints showed plainly in the sandy bottoms. Twice I had to circle when I lost them in the pines, and once I stopped to pick up a crumpled cigarette pack. Lucky Strikes. I put it in my pocket, mounted, and followed the tracks on, until they ended where I knew they would, at the empty portable pipe-corrals that Tanners' men had left behind.

20

Autumn had been on a long, sweet roll. In the meadows along Jackson Creek the aspen had completely turned; their dry leaves quivered in the light morning breeze like spotted yellow tinsel. Withered alsike clover sparkled each morning under melting frost, and when the frost burned away, it turned the bright green of Annie's emerald eyes. Stripped by the first storm, the alders rattled, stark and silver among the reds of wild rose and willow which had overgrown neglected portions of the meadows. And in the timber, pine tags turned an inviting warm tan.

On my knees, I watched as the old snag above me tipped, its brittle limbs twitching from the vibration of the saw, until, cut completely through, it stepped off its stump. As it fell, it pivoted a graceful quarter turn, seeming to hang for a moment, suspended between earth and sky.

I waited for the dust and flying sticks to settle, then climbed onto the butt and walked the length of the tree, limbing it close to the trunk with Harley's ancient Mall saw. Red rot churned from the teeth on the spinning chain and floated away on the exhaust. Straining against the weight and torque of the antique, gear-driven saw, I began to buck the log into fourteen-inch blocks.

The clean October light blued valleys below, yet seemed to amplify mountains rising along the horizon, light that intensified the reds and yellows in pine bark, magnifying the gemlike amber in each bead of pitch and sharpening the un-

likely Day-Glo colors of lichen clinging to the dark sides of
trees. Even the granite, that dull and most enduring feature
of the land, sparkled as light shot through its minerals,
flakes of mica sparkling like mirrors. I pulled off my shirt
and let the sun warm my back.

I sawed the stump flat for a chopping block and began
splitting wood. Elegantly simple, the work gave my hands
occupation and my mind a freedom to wander. The sky
above me seemed to crackle with light—as it had that October when she and I had headed south through the heart of
British Columbia, taking our time, towing her horse trailer
to the last, late shows of the season. Evenings we camped as
far from roads as we could, so taken with the country that
when we woke in the mornings, it was sometimes with a
sense of wonder—as we had near Revelstoke, encased in
cold nylon sleeping bags, shivering in the morning chill and
each other's heat, when we heard the first lonesome honks
and saw them coming in low over the lake, flying between
mist and the mirrorlike water, so close we could see their
eyes: the first fast flights of the migrating Canada geese.

I hadn't gone looking for war; it came to me that November, when Summer was shot down in the Highlands. In another month the light here would darken, trees would turn
dull again between the layered grays of stone and sky.

Calluses had formed along the base of my fingers. I could
feel strength coming back into my hands, strength so gradually reduced I'd only missed it after it had gone. I turned a
block so the fine crack across its top was opposite me and
drove the splitting maul through the barely visible line to the
heart. The stillness around me broke as blasts at the new
Kaiser quarry to the north echoed back off the Elkhorns.
Each day they drilled and dynamited further into the earth,
their charges reverberating from the hills. My hands ached
from the saw and maul, and I remembered that the grip I'd
had at twenty-two began to ebb at Fort Sill. "Hands-on
training," they called it, a faster way to make cannon cock-

ers, even though the war was winding down. Sergeant Major Lewis, cool and black as obsidian: *Run those ragheads out to the range their first day, put 'em on those guns, make them shoot till dark, then run 'em back here for chow.*

I split the wood fine, for Harley's kitchen range, and stacked the pieces carefully in the box of his pickup. Another distant blast rolled off the mountains, echoing back to me like the sergeant major's hip voice . . . *When they hit the classroom after that, they'll* KNOW *what the hell those level bubbles are for.* October, bright and fine, the worst of the killing summer heat behind us and a new training cycle under way. Ten nameless trainees standing in a nervous half-circle behind the split trails on my howitzer, facing me and Garrett on that open, sun-warmed Oklahoma hillside. Four complete batteries, trucks, a mess tent, commo wires running off through scrub oak to forward observer outposts. The hills we aim at would have been good to ride, low and rolling, open to sky.

The side of Harley's pickup had warmed in the sun. I rested my naked back against the metal, remembering how she was to have arrived that same day from Canada, remembering Garrett's hillbilly voice—*You better speak up, boy, when you're answerin' me*—as we started our new charges on basics, making them take turns—*COUNT OFF!*—burying the spades that anchor the gun against recoil. I show them one at a time how to place powder bags in the slim brass canisters, how to mount the sleek high-explosive projectiles on the canisters, how fuses are screwed into the hollow threaded noses of the projos, explaining how a clock in the fuse starts when the round is fired. And I tell them how the fuse determines exactly where a round explodes, how each fuse can be set to burst the charge aboveground or impact detonate when the projo strikes the ground; even be adjusted to delay until the projectile has buried itself underground. Bad guys in bunkers and spider holes don't much like that delayed fuse, I tell my trainees, and they grin, growing cocky already, beginning to believe.

Sweat trickled down my chest, although I hadn't moved in several minutes. *Stop. You can stop this right now.* But when it comes, it comes of itself, as if memory has a will of its own. My off-post running buddy and co-instructor, Drill Sergeant Billy Garrett, swinging into his act, harassing each new man from every sudden angle . . . *So don't be fumble-fartin' around dropping those fuses, you read me, boy? I said you HEAR me boy?!* . . . keeping them shook and awake, and when I good-cop them, they gravitate to me, listening and learning, anything to avoid his haunted eyes and lashing tongue.

She was coming to stay, and I had been in a frenzy of cleaning my off-post apartment, buying furnishings I wouldn't have bought for myself. Even as I elevate and traverse the barrel, spinning the cranks on the left side of the gun, I wonder where she is on the road. Garrett and I have the trainees level the gun bubbles over and over, until a cherry second lieutenant checks the piece with his gunnery quadrant, then off to one side asks me if he had the mills right. I explain the commands that will soon come: QUAD-RANT, how high; DEFLECTION, how wide; SHELL, high explosive, beehive, Willy Peter; FUSE, how long; CHARGE, how much powder. I show one man at a time how to push a complete round into the tube with a clenched fist, show him how the sliding breech block will actually push his fist away. "It will push your fist but not your fingers," I tell him. "Remember that or you'll be writing Jody left-handed letters." More tight grins as they carry projectiles in the crooks of their arms, each of them feeling the thrill of loading.

I shivered from the sweat chilled on my back and noticed wood chips scattered around the chopping block at my feet. *If only I had been paying attention, instead of thinking about you.* I touched the place where the purple scar ran along the side of my jaw. Off south, beyond the fields and timberline, as far away perhaps as the old Primm place, I heard a barking dog, then another and another.

We insert rubber earplugs and the world becomes deadly

and mute. The long delayed order for smoke comes; we cover our ears and open our mouths; one trainee on each of the sixteen howitzers rams a round into the breech, another runs the block closed, jerks the triggering lanyard, and we have rounds in the air. Every gun jumps, rubber tires bounce off the ground; recoil mechanisms flash back and the projectiles hurtle away: Look! You can see them! Brief dots against the October sky and they're gone in the ringing snap of stretched steel and the slamming impact of muzzle blast.

Dogs, running in the timber to the south, barking, frenzied, chasing something perhaps. Barking.

My trainees are stunned by the violence that is to become their craft. They look at each other like homesick boys. The rounds do not strike the ridge we watch but impact a mile beyond, where, finally, we see the faint trail of dust and smoke, and later hear what sounds like summer thunder. In three months those kids would have been good, good enough to hit a Vespa three miles away.

I listened to the dogs growing fainter, then bent, touched my toes a few times, and tried to shake the cramps from my trembling hands.

21

Even when you know you're avoiding trouble by staying away, the feeling that people in town are having secret fun haunts you in the hills. Town is always there, in the back of your mind, like a recurring dream of seduction, or your fear of death.

I'd grown up between two: Helena, where kids whose parents worked for the state government prowled the streets in gleaming cars, and Clancy, where people lived if they couldn't afford Helena.

When the gold had been dredged from the creeks and gouged from the hard-rock hills, after the Gregory smelter above Wicks closed and the miners moved, Clancy settled down as a third-rate ranch community, supported by the last wave of homesteaders—marooned there by hard times and distance. The Depression broke most of the ones who survived the horrors of influenza and hung on through winters like 1919. One bar lasted. If I had a hometown at all, that roadhouse made Clancy it.

I'd heard, although Smoke denied it, that he and Elmer Wallace had ridden saddle horses into a dance there one night, drunk as young lords; that a near riot followed, emptying dancers, drunks, and band members into the street. I'd heard this from men who swore they were there, and I liked the story, even if it wasn't true. I couldn't think of anyone my age who would still be around, but one Friday afternoon, after ricking my fifth load of wood in the wobble-floored log addition behind the kitchen, I stuffed a twenty-dollar bill in my jeans, tied my canvas coat to my saddle, and told Harley I was going to check the mail in Clancy, that I'd be home when I got home.

I rode across Schillings' grain fields and into the timbered hills, following my boyhood hunting trails past several long-abandoned homesteads. At Primm's, the door hung open on dry leather hinges; a few slender aspen grew through the broken board-and-batten roof. Primm had been a lonesome old man when Smoke was a child, and he had welcomed in the cold little boy my father had been, to warm up on his long cold walk to school.

The pole gate on the flat between Habb's and Mackin's leaned as if ready to fall down. Coyote carcasses, left by the government man as a warning or a brag, hung on the fence beside the gate. The coyotes had decayed; some had fallen in half, others seemed held together only by their hair, which riffled in the wind. I tightened my cinch a notch at the gate, avoiding their grinning, wasted faces.

Beyond Mackin's the burned-off hills came down to meet the town; the path of the wildfire, which Summer and I had watched from the bluffs above Harley's when we were kids, still plain upon the land.

Behind the Clancy Bar, in an overgrown field bordered by half-dead cottonwoods, I pulled my saddle and bridle and left the roan tied long in the dappled shade of the old trees so he could pick some grass and beat the late flies. I bought two packs of Camels at the overstocked general store, and looked around the long stone room. It smelled of fresh-cut beef and onions, rock candy and dry goods, soap and kerosene, depending on where you stood. Ray Swann nodded from his station beside the window as a lady I didn't know rang up my smokes.

"How are things up at your place, Mr. Swann?" I asked.

"Oh, fine, sure," he answered and lifted his withered hand. As I closed the door, I could almost hear Ray and the lady inside asking each other who I was.

At the post office, I opened Harley's box and pulled out an assortment of ranch catalogues, bills, and letters. There was an envelope for me too, postmarked Canada. I put my letter inside my shirt, army style.

Outside, kids walked and ran past, coming from the red-brick school beyond the store. And for a moment I was among them, small again, wearing my belted mackinaw and scuffed, high-top shoes, pushing and getting shoved, throwing rocks and running. They passed as I'd once passed, with Mr. Swann watching now, as then, through the store window. I walked on, down the empty street toward a beer sign that blinked: IT'S THE WATER.

The bar was empty except for an old couple snuggled together at a corner table. I had a shot with a beer back and fed quarters into the jukebox, playing a song that Summer had liked while he'd been home on leave, between his tours overseas. The words followed me back to the stools where we had listened to them then: "Drove my Chevy to the levee, but the levee was dry/The good ol' boys were drinking whiskey and rye, singing, 'This'll be the day that I die.'"

"That's us," Summer said. "You and me, just good old boys." He shook his head in a way he'd picked up from Harley, listening to words I guessed he understood. He'd already flown a tour over there, he knew what he was going back to, and he drank like there was no tomorrow. "Promise me this, Jack," he'd said, his words running together, his eyes finding mine in the whiskey haze between us. "Stick around until I get back. Stick around and keep an eye on the old guys."

Mr. Swann entered and got his silent glass of beer at the bar. He watched the little town year after year and probably knew specifics that wives and husbands wouldn't discover until their divorce proceedings. Without a word, he'd find out who I was too.

I arranged my change and cigarettes and spread my hands on the familiar wood of the bar. The Beam went down hot and hard, smoothed by the chaser into a radiance of daydreams and that certain clarity which sometimes follows your second shot. I remembered how I'd planned to come home, how I'd planned to get off the bus at the edge of town and walk in, sharp in my winter greens, sergeant's stripes, and citations. I smiled at that distant barracks dream, long dead and only by accident remembered. I tapped out a Camel and fiddled with it on the bar. I had pulled my share of Friday nights in here, but I'd never been a regular. It would have been a letdown if I'd let that lonesome expectation live.

I took off my hat. It was dusty and sweat-stained around the band, almost to the point where the crown would crack, when felt took on the rich quality of soiled leather. I watched the air rise in my beer, each bubble isolated from the others, but all eventually rising to break on the surface. And part of me knew I was off and gone again, that, as with Smoke when he'd been running, anything could happen; almost certainly, if something could go wrong, it would.

"Just keep smilin', you nigger," someone said and laid a powerful hand on my shoulder. I turned slowly, and there, dressed in a dirty lace-up buckskin shirt, wheat jeans, and loggers, bearded halfway to his belt, stood Wilderness Foamy.

I held out my hand. "Hey, Bug! How they hanging?"

"Shittin' in high cotton," Foamy answered and bore down on my fingers. Skintight and gaunt, Wilderness Foamy, pound for pound, was the strongest man I'd ever met. We'd started calling him Wilderness when he dropped out of the eighth grade to live alone and wild in an isolated prospector's shack near the snowbound Caterac Basin. By the time I finished high school, Wilderness had become an expert trapper, packer, and poacher. He was known then to sometimes walk thirty miles a day in the mountains, never to be seen unless he wanted to be seen. "You out of the army?" he asked and waved at Clarence, the bartender. He saw the scar and slash of white hair, and an uncommon respect touched his voice. "Heard you had some trouble."

"I got banged up. What are you doing in town?"

"Livin' here. Me and the brothers and the old man."

"Say again, over?" I felt the whiskey burning in my face, heard it in the echo of my voice.

"Yeah, uh-huh. Got into the building trades. Making the fucking dinero too. Building back-country hunting lodges and like that. Hard on you though." Foamy lifted the thin buckskin shirt to reveal a back brace. His eyes swept the room in a continual search for prey or hidden ambush.

"Do you still have that silver badger?"

"Naw. He run off. Long time ago now. Chasing badger pussy, I guess. Rank anyway, him around the shack like that, scratching and pissin' all the time." Wilderness kept his back to the bar. His eyes continued their restless patrol of the room even as he drank.

"Building cabins where?" I asked.

He snapped his pale eyes to me for an instant. "Up in the Cateracs," he answered.

"That put a cramp on your country?"

"Naw," he said and turned his glass upside down on the pitted bar. "Snowmobilers burn a couple down every winter, you know? Keeps us going real steady."

22

I noticed that my stack of dollar bills had dwindled. The stools along the bar had sprouted people, and the volume of noise had evolved from the white hum of afternoon conversation to the rolling hammer mill of after-work Friday night fun. I looked around the room, decided it was time to head home, and ordered a last beer, while trying to ignore a man beside me who spoke with an accent I knew all too well. "So this *after*noon," he was saying, "we drove up and looked at it. Crik or no crik, it surely ain't worth no eight grand an acre."

"Just what the neighborhood needs," I said to Clarence when he handed me the beer. "Okies." I guess the whiskey put an edge on my voice I hadn't meant. Folks in Oklahoma had treated me fine. From the corner of my eye, I saw the man beside me turn and look me over. I took hold of the icy bottle and straightened a little at a time.

"Kiss *my* ass and call me Mildred if *I'm* an Okie," he said, turning slowly too, as if we were partners, dancing a subdued and ritualistic prelude to some later rock and roll. A square-shouldered, bull-necked man of about forty, with well-trimmed graying hair, he looked at me from hooded eyes set deep in a forehead that reminded me of a Durham bull. Clarence lingered with my dollar bill in his hand, watching with an expert's eye. "What'll it be?" he asked my new friend.

"*Tall* CC ditch with a water back. And another *tall* one for the linguist here."

"West Texas then," I said, smiling in spite of the sure knowledge that one of us was headed for the door.

"Not bad," he said, his eyes moving deliberately from my jaw to the white line of hair. "Pretty good ear. So what's this Okie shit?"

I tightened my grip on the bottle. "My mistake. How's White Trash sound?"

To my surprise, he laughed. An honest, husky laugh with no meanness or quarter asked in it. He looked at me, rubbed his forehead with the fingers of his right hand, and said, "Pretty close." He took off his glasses and set them on the bar, and I got ready to slip the haymaker I knew was coming. Instead, he lifted his drink and looked me over again. "You just get out of the military or something?"

I nodded, and he said, "Uh-huh. Got GI stamped all over you." He paused, then with a sincerity I found hard to resist, said, "Besides, you look like the day after a Hanoi Super Bowl."

I pegged him for a retired first sergeant, relaxed, and leaned back against the bar on my elbows. "When were you there?"

"'Sixty-three and 'sixty-four. Sixteen months in the Delta. Came home with the clap and an ass full of scar tissue. We were advisers then, remember?"

"You didn't go back?"

"Go back, shit!" he said. "Soon as I got my stitches out, I headed for summer camp at Green Bay as a free agent. Got cut. Finally played Canadian league that season."

I turned to get my drink and noticed a midget sitting on the bar on the far side of the Texan. "Hey, there's a midget," I said.

"Oh yes. These are my regressive sons." He pointed to the midget. "This is Bean. You can tell him because he's always underfoot. And Young Arthur, our class act," he pointed behind him down the bar, to a dark young man who flashed us a smile, "because *he's* always someplace else." The Texan fluttered one hand and giggled like an aging fullback on nitrous oxide. I felt myself smiling again, and this time it felt all right.

"Don't pay any attention to *him,*" Bean said, climbing to his feet on the bar and walking toward me like a ruptured bulldog. "We've promised him some drugs if he behaves himself." He was the ugliest person I'd ever seen, except maybe for an alcoholic coastal Indian I once noticed sleeping off a drunk on a muddy street in Woodpecker, British Columbia.

"He used to be much taller," the Texan whispered. "Total moral disintegration. Don't look too closely or you'll upset him, and he gets nasty, let me tell you, when he's upset."

Young Arthur, on the other hand, looked like a 1930s Hollywood star, his hair parted toward the center of his head, a carefully trimmed Clark Gable mustache, and a studied, devil-may-care expression on his tanned, handsome face. He held up his drink; it had olives in it. "Pango Pango," he told me.

"And I'm Duncan Carlisle, linebacker for several professional teams you've probably never heard of and spiritual guide for these misshapen youths." The bearlike man sighed and held out his hand.

As we shook I said, "You're looking for land?"

"Just for a cabin—place to work with enough privacy to piss off the *front* porch."

I thought of Wilderness Foamy but hesitated.

"He's a writer now," Bean said, his ruined face bobbing on his stumpy neck. "Too old for football and too drunk to fuck most of the time. He doesn't mean any harm, poor toady old fart."

"That's no way to talk about the man who deserted you before you were born," Carlisle said, indignantly shaking his load of worried silver hair. "Confidentially," he confided, "we're on a quest. We're searching for my third son, Little Orris, who is supposed to have been seen near here, sleeping in cars. He's AWOL from navy welding school, you know."

"What does he look like?"

"Oh, I haven't any idea," Carlisle answered. "I deserted him too, of course. But, you see, we've heard he's come into some money." He giggled, raised his fingers again to his forehead, and with mock shrewdness, studied my features. "*You* aren't Little Orris, are you?"

"I don't guess I'd be sleeping in cars if I'd just come into some money."

"Well, that's *right*. Of course not. I'll tell you, friend, as head of a broken chain of broken families and as inspirational King Kong of the Von Trash Family Singers, I struggle against tremendous odds. Like not being able to figure out simple shit like *that*. The genetic backlash of my offspring here, and trying to find Little Orris while managing them, has affected my mind."

Clarence brought a round and Carlisle paid absently by sweeping several bills toward the inside of the bar with the back of his hand.

"Something's affected his mind all right," Bean said and winked. "Something white he keeps putting in his nose."

I thanked Carlisle for the drink, but he didn't seem to notice. He was writing in a pocket notebook with urgent and obvious concentration. Bean and Young Arthur discovered the NO GUNS IN THE BAR sign, and I turned back to my beer, remembering the ride home.

Carlisle touched my elbow with the notebook. "Writing has harmed my mind too," he said, his forehead wrinkled like a great fist. "This is my poem for this *after*noon."

In large, child's letters, I made out the printed words: MORE DRUGS.

I slid it back. "Pretty short," I said. "Maybe you should try longer lines."

Duncan Carlisle lifted the lid on a Balkan Sobranie cigarette tin with his finger. "We can discuss prosody, or we can just go outside and do some longer lines."

I didn't seem to have noticed how much the place had

crowded up, and I was surprised, as we pushed our way toward the door, by the number of well-dressed young people. I'd always thought of the Clancy Bar as a backwater, hillbilly joint. Not a hideaway for preppy young professionals in elbow-patched tweeds. But then, I'd been gone.

The evening had turned off mild. Sunset, still a half hour off, had begun to color the western sky beyond the stump-peppered, burned-off hills, an intense spectrum of vibrating blues. We walked past the post office and on into a field between town and the railroad tracks.

"Great old bar," Bean said, toddling along with one hand clasped to Carlisle's sleeve for balance. "Reminds me of the Turf in Missoula."

"Awfully clean, though. What this area really needs is a few good dumps," Young Arthur said, "creeping landfills among the pines, compactors, methane, attendants selected because they were once Nazi dentists."

"Most folks around here use prospect holes," I said.

Young Arthur's expression darkened. "Private dumps?"

I stopped, took my turn on the coke Carlisle had lined in the lid of the tiny tin box. "Sure. Some of these old mine shafts have eighty feet of tin cans in them."

"Tubular landfills! Put that up your nose, Carlisle," Bean piped, rolling into a handstand and taking a few lurching steps before collapsing in a weak puddle of thrashing limbs.

We walked along the railroad tracks beside the brush-lined banks of the Little Prickly Pear, listening to freighters changing gears on the Interstate, and to Carlisle ramble about his clapboard, migrant childhood in Texas, where there had been nothing permanent, nothing pretty, and nothing to go back for; about years of playing injured and the exposé he'd later written on bush-league football; about the popularity of the book and the novels that had followed; about his month-long high-speed drives around the West and how he always ended up back in Montana. "I envy you this country to come home to," he said. "When I got out,

Green Bay was as much home to me as anywhere else in this wasteland."

"I'm not going to stay," I told him. "There's nothing here for me. I'll be heading for Canada in a couple of weeks."

"Well, Frostbacks are fine, but I'll tell you"—he paused, the fingers again rising to touch his forehead—"when I'm somewhere else, I get homesick for Montana. And—as you know—I'm not even fucking *from* here."

Like most of the other things about him I noticed, his abrupt sincerity kept catching me off balance. He talked like a Klan Grand Dragon, but here we were firing up a doobie to smooth us out, while he congratulated me on being from a place I figured most strangers forgot by the time they got to the outskirts of Helena. He took a long hit and we strolled on in silence until he let out the smoke with a giggle. "Lately," he continued, "the Von Trash family has taken to holding services at out-of-the-way western dumps. Although, of course, we do attend the major landfills, for communion with the masses, small dumps are our forte. Eugene here is our dump deacon. Handles vestments and seating."

The three of them broke up, high and rolling, running well-worn material that for me wore well. I laughed too, imagining the Errol Flynn–like Young Arthur in some sort of Iron Age bogeyman cloak, hooded like a ninth-century Irish monk, praying to a Caterpillar as it dozed beer cans and tampons into the Stinking Pit of No Return. Garbage, at that moment, seemed a reasonable thing to worship—the end of all our struggles, the residue of our ambitions and greed. It didn't matter why they had hit upon and worked out their routine. The laughter mattered; I understood this, and as we walked on down the tracks, past the spot where Harley's father had stepped deliberately in front of a high-balling steam engine, we laughed until we hurt.

23

In the arabesques and phantoms of evening light, we walked back to the bar, good old boys, talking pocket-knives, pickup trucks, and fishing trips. For a moment we stood in the street and admired the crafty outer staircase that led to a seemingly empty upstairs above the bar, speculating on the original intent of such arrangements. Inside, we worked our way through the crowd to our places. Our money still lay beside our warm drinks; the bar clock had spun to eight forty-five.

I looked for "American Pie" on the juke again, but couldn't find it in the blur of labels. I dropped in some quarters and punched numbers. "I've got to get out of here," I said to myself, then glanced up to see if anybody had noticed my moving lips. Someone had. Sitting with several other women dressed in skirts and blouses, their hair uniformly spray-gunned into place with double-formula acetone, a streaked driftwood blond raised her glass an eighth of an inch and smiled. I tipped my hat as western as I could, and, keeping my good side toward her, turned back to the jukebox. The green selection light was still on.

I forced myself to read and punched Roy Orbison's "Pretty Woman." She appeared as the light went out, dressed in expensive fibers, nylons, and heels. She arched one eyebrow as she looked me over. "Hi, cowboy," she said.

"You bet. It doesn't hurt once in a while."

"What?" she asked, a smile playing on her electric lips.

Divorced and employed, in her late thirties, out showing her stuff with the girls, she wasn't about to back off. Roy Orbison obligingly moaned behind me.

"Cowboy songs. I just played one for you."

"That's sweet," she said. Her friends gave us their sidelong and undivided attention.

"Would you like to dance?" I felt myself swaying and tried to stop by widening my stance.

"Don't be silly," she said. "In here?"

"On the porch?"

She stared at me, seeming actually to think it over.

"Or," I wavered and leaned against the juke, "I could show you my horse."

Her lips twitched at the corners of her cruel little mouth. "You don't waste any time, do you?"

"I've wasted enough already."

"Listen." She cocked her head on one shoulder and looked into my eyes. "Would you—"

"Excuse me," Carlisle said. "But this man is under investigation by the VTFS. He really shouldn't be talking to you this way." He turned me toward the bar, and when I looked back, she was standing beside the juke, one hand on her hip, the tight little smile still twisting her lips. "We didn't want to interrupt a beautiful moment, but we're heading for the Modern West," Carlisle said. "You want to ride in with us?"

"The Modern West?"

"Well, that settles *that*," Carlisle chortled.

"It's a redneck joint in Helena," Bean said. "Something between the Augusta Rodeo and World War III."

It sounded pretty good, so I explained about the horse. After listening attentively, Carlisle said, "Well, of course you've got to come with us. It's the only thing you can do. Take your horse home and we'll meet you there."

I drew a rough map for them and warned them to kill their lights and wait for me at the red gate. I bought a twelve-pack of Rainier, handed it to Young Arthur, and asked Clarence for an unopened road beer for myself. I told them it would take me an hour and left them leaning peacefully along the bar, their sense of urgent departure seemingly gone.

Frost was falling in the thin night air as I untied my canvas coat from the saddle. The roan snorted, and in the dim light of the distant street I watched jets of vapor pump from his nostrils. I slipped into the coat, grateful to find my worn gloves stuffed in the pockets. I put Harley's mail in the deep inside cigar pocket and buttoned the coat around me.

The horse yanked back and tried to rear as I laid the pad on his back. I got my right arm over his neck and struggled to hang on. Around the cottonwood tree he went, jumping sideways, dragging me like a doll. I knew I should have shortened his tether and let him smell the blanket before fooling with him in the dark, and I wondered, as I skipped along, hugging his neck and trying to keep away from his flying front feet, why I hadn't.

He stopped, trembling and tense. I let go of him, and we stood, our foreheads almost touching, eyeing each other. He smelled me and nickered, low in his throat, then bumped my face with his nose.

I hunted up the saddle pad again and very slowly worked at getting him saddled. I could feel the nerves in him jumping through his muscles and the blood jetting through his veins. A harvest moon rose the width of a young girl's hand above the black bulk of the Elkhorns. I watched it climb the sky, glad to have its light.

On the county road, I turned the stirrup toward me and took a deep breath. The roan took off in a businesslike trot; I gradually found the off stirrup with my boot, and we went along smooth, his action fine, covering ground with each swinging stride. I popped open the road beer. It foamed down my hand and onto the horse's neck, and it tasted better than its predecessors when I raised it to my lips, the malty smell of it sharp in the crisp night air.

I decided to take the frontage road to the old Saint 'Amour place rather than go back through Mackin's. Half as many gates, shorter, and I hadn't been over that way yet. It would be a pretty ride once we got away from the road and into the moon-shadowed, piney woods. The deserted Saint 'Amour homestead had been my hunting ground in the days when Summer and I bet a dollar a point on horns. It had been what *Field & Stream* would call "A Big Buck Bonanza."

As I swung the roan through the intersection between the bar and store, I heard a woman in the direction of the parking lot say, "Look!" Someone started a compact car and swung it around until the lights were in our eyes. I felt the roan lift his tail, heard the plop of muffins hitting asphalt. The little car swerved past us, blowing its muted horn. I hung on as the roan's hooves slid and rattled on the pavement. A woman's shrill laughter floated back to me, punctuated by the snap of breaking glass. The roan plowed into a darkness spotted by green and red splotches of light that reminded me of night-fire dots, yet we both knew the runaway was mostly make-believe.

Gradually my vision returned and I made out the grass-lined borrow pit alongside the road, the barbed wire fence that flanked it, and the moonlit, boulder-littered country ahead. Carlisle the poet, I mused and remembered a poem I'd been assigned to read in college, a long one that I never finished. I pulled on my gloves, remembering how, early in the poem, a drunken young man rides a thoroughbred stud off a California coastline cliff into the sea.

Two miles later, in the miniature hills around the remnants of Saint 'Amour's log house and barn, I found the blue glow of mercury-vapor lights burning among the trees. A dog barked, then another and another. Someone, I discovered as I rode up a newly dozed road, had built several dozen houses right in the heart of my big-buck hot spot. I should have known better than to mix snow and weed and whiskey; the old Boone and Crockett quality bucks didn't seem any more possible right then than blue yard lights or the thunder of surf breaking in the meadows below. I let the roan walk and waited out a dizzy, nauseating sense of falling.

Of course no one was at the red gate when I got there. I left Harley a note with his mail, picked up my Prince Albert can of army drug goodies, a hundred dollars mad money, and my best boots. For something to do, I walked on, past the gate and up the lane through the timber, marveling at the urges that drive us; here I was, old Sergeant Solitude, waiting for three guys I'd never seen before, to go barrel-assing off to a honky-tonk in the middle of the night. And actually hoping they'd show.

The road was covered with a thin layer of dried pine tags, softened by frost. I walked on, quiet, listening to owls booming their horny questions from the bluffs behind the barn. It was an odd imbalance, I knew, my fear of town and the absolute need to periodically return to test it. Hadn't Annie made a point of my staying out here too much? She knew life, and I chose to believe that knowledge gave her courage as well.

At the far edge of the timber, I heard poles rattle in the cattle guard. A car growled softly down through the trees, and as if from beyond the cold moon overhead, the sound of Carlisle's laughter drifted into the pines from the moonstruck prairie beyond. What the hell, I thought. This one's for Summer.

We blasted through the night in the open Caddy convertible Carlisle called the Dumpster, drinking beer and laughing while he drove with the headlights off. By the time we got to Montana City, they had decided I was Little Orris after all, and maybe because they didn't know my real name, Orris stuck. Carlisle drove with a sure hand, as if he'd driven that back road to town all his life.

24

From the ornate elevated bar, we watched the bright confusion of couples jitterbugging to a loudly efficient Country-Western band. Strobe lights shot sparks off multi-faceted globes twirling overhead. Bystanders whooped and waved while the dancers flung themselves against the music. In one corner of the barn-sized room, a mechanical bull lurched and spun, pitching one rider after another into the circle of western-attired onlookers, who cheered and booed and called for more victims. I noticed Annie dancing with a man I didn't know, locked for an instant in his arms, then swinging away, her eyes bright in the flashing, multicolored light. The scene reminded me of a much different dance, one we'd attended at an old-fashioned, false-fronted community hall in New Denver, British Columbia, on the last Saturday night in October. Long-haired young woodspeople had come in from the mountains to play, and we joined them, as we happened to be there, on our slow trip south. That night, standing outside the dance hall, listening to a string band play "Rock Me on the Water," I had lit a cigarette with my draft card.

I slipped the Prince Albert can from my pocket. Army pharmaceuticals, mules were for night fire, when you had to stay sharp without jitters. One kept you awake for twenty-four hours. Two kicked your ass. I took a couple. The whiskey I washed them down with reminded me of buckles I'd almost won, of parking lots and go-cups, of forgotten stretches of dusty back roads and jackpot towns. That pure sharp taste called back a confusion of nights and miles, regained with clarity and lost again in a flickering instant.

A beer sign triptych turned waterfalls into rivers and the rivers into lakes above the fancy back bar; drinkers crowded the deck above the dance floor as hostility and cigarette smoke clouded the room. For years this had been Smoke's domain: honky-tonks and Saturday-night dances in country schools, pool halls, and country bars. He had run hard and paid high. When he stopped, it seemed he'd tried to make it up to Summer and me by working himself half to death. From nowhere the notion struck me that he may have loved us; that out of shyness or a lack of grace, perhaps, he hadn't been able to let us know. The idea sobered me as I thought of him and the years, like Harley, he'd spent alone. Then the night pulled me back toward satin shirts and high-crowned hats and hard-breasted girls only an arm's length away.

I tried the iron bull, seeing in the signature I signed on the release form just how far gone I truly was. I lasted maybe three seconds and landed on my back. The room turned slowly on an invisible axis, Annie put her arm around my waist, and I grinned into her fine green eyes.

"I went eight seconds on number six, you sorry outfit," she said, giving me a squeeze.

"You have a date, Annie?"

"Well, sure. What? You land on your head?"

"I fall to pieces," I said in her ear.

"Sure, Scooter, I know. Let me walk you back to your buddies before you fall *over*." She circled my waist again with her arm, and we made for the bar like young landowners in love.

"Another time, another race," I told her.

"You count on it," she answered and left me leaning at the bar. I stood dreaming past nights and better rides until I noticed the familiar black hair and leather jacket gliding among the dancers. Carlisle and his boys had adjourned to a card room. I gunned a shot and headed through the tables after her.

I tapped the man she was dancing with on the shoulder, meaning to cut in. He turned and I forgot about dancing. He stared at me, then grinned as he had that day at the dredge pond. I stared back and felt the mules kick into overdrive.

"Well, if it isn't the trespasser," he said. As he started to laugh, I picked him up by his belt and pearl-buttoned shirt and dropped him ass-first on the nearest table. He came off the floor like a cat—amid the screams and curses of the people whose table had disappeared—all cables and reflex, quick and hard, like Summer had been. The calm that's supposed to back up the mules didn't come.

So many people grabbed us that we seemed to float through the open door. Store signs and streetlights threw slanting shadows across the dim parking lot, highlighting and hiding at the same time the crowd we drew. The cowboy's buddies yelled polite encouragement as we circled each other. "Tear his fuckin' guts out, Steve," one of them called again and again.

His left came in so fast I didn't see it. Somebody behind me yelled, "Get some!" and he did, landing another clean shot above my eye. I knew I was too far gone to worry about hand speed, so I concentrated on keeping away from him. The lefts came again and again. Hitting me didn't seem to be a problem as I stumbled back, and he warmed to the crowd. I held my forearms together in front of my face, as Ali had in his last fights, and I noticed that in spite of everything, he was still wearing his damn hat.

"Hey! Come on, for Christ's sake, he's drunk!" I heard Annie say as she tried to come through the circle of onlookers. Someone grabbed her from behind and pulled her back. I dropped my hands and caught one flush on the bone above my eye.

I jerked my hands back up, wondering why, with my elbows so high, he didn't try to work my body. I picked off a couple shots and noticed how he dropped his shoulders and leaned in for leverage just before he threw the jab.

Showboating.

I switched to a right lead, circling to my right, hoping to slip a few. The jab came right on schedule. As I shifted back to the left lead, he threw his right. For a second I heard burlap tear inside my head; from a far-off place, panic sang to my heart.

I worked left, wiping blood from my eye with the back of my hand. I felt my legs coming back and picked up the pace, lowering my hands as he seemed to slow down. My eyes cleared, and I saw the front of his ripped shirt, flapping above his belt, saw how he dipped and ducked his head, slipping imaginary punches. When he dropped his shoulder to throw the crowd-pleaser, I stepped in, bent my right knee, and drilled a counter-right over his oncoming left. I threw it from my toes, from my knees and hips, with every ounce of strength I could find in my body. My fist struck bone. I followed with a left, hooking for his short ribs, but he was already going down. My momentum carried me a step, and I fell right on him.

We rolled apart. I sat back on my heels and rested. The crowd quieted, and in the far-off night I heard a distant siren. On our knees, we leaned against each other. He straightened and clubbed me on the cheek. I took hold of his shirt collar with my left hand and hit him three short rights, catching his teeth each time his head snapped back. He wasn't wearing the Resistal any longer, and the grin was gone.

He swayed against me and tried to sucker me with an uppercut. I slipped it and noticed a pack of cigarettes lying on the pavement between us. Lucky Strikes. I pushed him back, and for the first time felt real anger rising in my heart. "Remember this the next time you roust an old man," I said, and broke his nose.

I knew I couldn't stand to hit him again, so I pushed him

over backward. Someone grabbed my jacket, pulled me to my feet, and hustled me across the parking lot. I shook loose and in the light of a carpet barn across the lot saw it was Carlisle.

"Let's go," he said. "Before the heat gets here."

I looked back and saw Sandy Martinez kneeling beside the man named Steve. She held his hat, but I doubted he knew she was there. We ran, ducking around back in time to see Bean jumping up and down on the Dumpster's front seat. Young Arthur vaulted into the back, and holding my hat high, he howled at the waning moon.

As we drove lightless down back alleys, Carlisle looked over at me. "Way to go, Orris. I especially liked the way you wore him down by beating up his hands with your face." He chuckled to himself. "You did real good on your knees though. Boy, you surely did."

My lips felt like raw link sausage. I tried to smile without moving them.

"Better pull around to the ER at Saint Peter's," Bean said to Carlisle, his flat little face tilted into the slipstream of icy air boiling off the windshield. "Way he's bleeding, this dude's gonna take some stitches."

25

I woke in a sweat-soaked army blanket on a red shag carpet, half under a dining-room table. I crawled out, got to my feet, and looked for a bathroom. A purse, woman's shoes, and underwear lay scattered in a trail across the carpet and into the kitchen, as if the owner had undressed on the run. Beer cans, whiskey bottles, and overflowing ashtrays littered the sink and yellow Formica countertops. I picked up a few cans until I found a nearly full one, then wandered into the adjoining bathroom.

I did not take heart at what I saw in the mirror. My face was puffy and bruised, the left eye black, most of the eyebrow snipped away and stitched. There was dried blood in my ear, on my neck, my shirt, and T-shirt. And there was red lint in my hair. I noticed a blue-green goose egg on the back of my right hand, which hurt when I moved my fingers.

I ran cold water on the hand, then dunked my head under the tap. I began to shake and sat down on the cool linoleum floor, resting my back against the commode. A hand appeared above the rim of the tub; the shower curtain rattled back to reveal a young woman, naked as a fawn, up to her neck in bubble bath. She yawned and pulled the curtain closed as if I wasn't there.

After the first waves of hangover panic washed through me, I gunned the rest of the beer and limped back to the living room. I found my wallet in one boot, a near-full can of beer in the other. My coat covered someone I didn't know next to the front door.

Outside, the weather had fouled; the sky rode low, heavy and gray as wet cement on the horizon. I looked back at the house as I walked away. Tall and narrow, done in yellow plaster and white trim, it looked safe and sane. Through the trees along the street, I could see the red plastic *K* of the Helena K mart store over on Moccasin Flat. The Dumpster was nowhere in sight.

I walked along the county road, my hands deep in my pockets, feeling with each step the throb of blood behind my eyes. Had it really happened, or had I only dreamed—as I had dreamed so many other things—that in the emergency room, on the other side of a corrugated divider, they had set his nose while I was being sewn up, that I had seen his boots under the edge of the curtain as he wept?

An antelope whistled on a ridge ahead. Only the white rumps of the little band kept me from missing them on the yellowed hillside as they ran ghostlike toward the skyline. My life seemed as directionless as theirs, their flight mine. Why else, after so much time and all my carefully laid plans, was I again living like a boy under Harley's roof, why else would I face him like a kid caught fighting at school, instead of finding the courage to leave?

I rounded a corner above Bell's cabin and saw a dump truck and low-boy trailer parked ahead off the road. Above me, on the low, contoured flank of Harris Hill, a Caterpillar dozer cut grade through the buffalo trails. It was surprising how easily the ground yielded under the blade, how dark and rich the soil seemed, exposed beneath the yellowed native grass.

.   .   .

The buildings were padlocked, so I took the brass key ring from under the eave, let myself in, and built a fire in the Windsor stove. I filled a pan with water and placed it on the lid to heat and wondered who Annie had been with the night before. With my back to the warming stove, I studied Harley's wall of memories. Aged and graying photographs of men in torn work clothes standing proud beside old cars; threshing crews, uniformly dressed in bib overalls, forking bundles into stationary threshers; Smoke, a little boy sporting a Jackie Coogan haircut, the knees out of his jeans, holding a cottontail rabbit high with one hand and a single-shot .22 rifle in the other; my grandmother, her black hair done in slender braids, dying of cancer. Four generations of crude trophies: Harley's saddle and quirt, the bull-riding buckles Summer had brought home, a wooden whistle carved like a bird that Smoke had won in a long-ago horserace, and my grandma's father's wooden shoes. There I was too, maybe four years old, my hands filled with the unkempt mane hair of a proud-cut, sway-backed Belgian workhorse. My legs stick straight out on his broad back and I'm grinning like an idiot boy. Perhaps that's right where the trouble had started, a forgotten moment on an idle afternoon, over twenty years before, when the long, slow pull that had brought me back began.

The pan rocked on the stove. I took off my shirt, and the crumpled letter fluttered to the floor. I left it where it fell as I dunked my head in the pan, lathered my neck and face and arms. Someone must have held the lead rope so the old horse would stand for the picture. That would certainly have been Harley. But who had snapped the camera? Smoke? Summerfield? My mother? I dried slowly with a rough towel, patted my face lightly, and decided not to shave. I buttoned on a fresh work shirt and put the letter back against my belly.

From the house, the blind corral seemed an odd confusion of weather-grayed lumber and freshly peeled raw wood. The cows and calves I'd caught grazed in the meadows; the roan napped on three legs in his spot beside the barn. Smoke's Walker stood in some aspen at the creek. The old place was at peace; as I stepped into the chill of the oncoming storm, the lonesome serenity of hills and meadows washed through me and seemed to leave me clean.

On a whim, I rolled open the long shop door and poked around in the random litter of tools and machinery that covered the floor. The smell of cold iron and decaying Marfac grease filled my swollen nose. Broken mower pitmans, pump jacks, harrow bars, and bent plow beams lay piled around a pedal-driven emery wheel.

Against one wall, resting on flat tires, stood Harley's motorcycle. I straddled the dusty 1939 Harley-Davidson and sat down on the stiff, spring-loaded seat. It was where his nickname had started, why Annie called me Scooter. I clunked the gearshift alongside the gas tank and bounced the rigid front shocks. I'd ridden the county roads—cow trails too—learning the country from the back of the old machine while hanging tight to Harley's flapping shirt.

For years the emery wheel had stood in the wood yard behind the house. On it I'd sharpened barrel bands and rusty ax heads into the swords and halberds of my boyhood war dreams. I remembered pumping the wheel around and around, the sparks flying up in an arc toward the house, and once, outlined for an instant through my parabola of star bursts, I remembered seeing Harley and Amy at the kitchen window, looking out, and holding each other.

The cattle lifted their white faces as I walked among them. Remnants of years of careful toil, they grazed along in peace. I spoke to them. They belched and chewed and watched me with calm eyes. The houseboat named *Mabel* lay on its side in the rocks where it seemed to have landed after a flood. The idea appealed to me, but there probably wasn't enough water in Jefferson County to float the old hulk.

I sat on a stump at the edge of the field and took the letter from my shirt. There was my name, written in her even yet ornate hand.

Dear Jack,
It seems we aren't meant to be together this fall, as if we've never been meant to be together. I understand your concern for your family, but it doesn't ease the disappointment I feel as days slip by.

The way things are, I feel a need to find something— perhaps a job—to help pass the time. I simply *can't* stay here any longer, waiting, waiting, waiting.

I don't mean to sound bitter, and you know I'm not, but for now I need to put myself in a new place, meet some new people, maybe learn some new tricks. I'll let you know what I've decided just as soon as *I* know.

Decided against the gelding I wrote about.
Mr. Kittredge hired a new man last week.
Love,

I folded the letter carefully and watched as clouds like boiling lead churned across the sky. The creek gasped beneath the roots of cottonwoods; alders rattled dry as bones in the rising wind. If I'd been paying attention that day on the range at Sill, instead of thinking about her driving down, if I'd been thinking about what I was doing instead of hurrying, none of this would be happening. If only—I touched my eyebrow, feeling the swelling along the bone—I'd kept that promise to Summerfield.

I sat on the stump and watched the cattle and wondered how long I would survive the stalking town, which, since we'd chosen not to live there, seemed now to be coming to us.

— 26 —

Harley put both hands to his mouth and whistled the shrill, complex whistle I'd never been able to learn. I stood, looked toward the house, and he waved me to his news.

Sometime that morning, probably as I was walking the highway home, a station wagon had driven up Amy's road, then off across her front field to within twenty yards of the house. Several casually dressed men got out and began walking around, gesturing in the direction of her buildings, and talking among themselves.

Seeing them from her sun porch, where she was doing the week's laundry and watching the dozer on Harris Hill with her binoculars, Amy opened the screen door, shaded her eyes, and asked the men what they wanted. When they ignored her and continued to glance from papers toward her out buildings, Amy retreated inside. Annie hadn't come home from the night before, and Amy, alone and uncertain about what was happening, pulled a Model 97 Winchester pump shotgun from her hall closet, along with the only box of shells she had—some No. 4 paper-wrapped duck loads a dozen years old. Painfully, she removed the plug from the tubular magazine with her stiff fingers and snapped five rounds through the magazine trap at the bottom of the action. She placed five more rounds in her apron pocket, put on her straw hat, and walked outside.

The men had bunched near the front of their vehicle and

were studying a map by the time Amy entered her fenced-in garden. She walked to the board fence with the shotgun out of sight and told the men that they were trespassing, that they'd better get out of her hay field or tell her what they were doing, and pretty damn sudden. They looked up, glanced at each other, and resumed talking in low voices.

Amy hoisted the pump gun onto the fence. The first round cleaned most of the window glass from the passenger-side door, peppered the plastic magnetized sign, and speckled one corner of the windshield. Too stunned by the blast to move, the men coveyed together like quail, except for one, who caught a wild pellet in the thigh. He ran a few steps, then limped in a tight circle and spoke with God.

Amy had to use both hands to ratchet another quacker load into the chamber. She braced up, gritted her teeth, and blew the gracefully curved rear side window away. Pieces of glass and torn shreds of headliner flew about gaily inside the rocking vehicle. "I mean business now," Amy grunted, as she rested the stock on the ground in order to pump another round into the chamber. She wiped away tears that the pain of recoil had put in her eyes and lifted the Model 97 again. The well-heeled men broke into a shameless sprint across the field, their arms flapping as if toward flight, for the safety of the county road.

She cut loose the third round several feet over their bobbing heads at a distance of eighty yards, and the running men leaped and swatted at themselves as if they'd just been run down by an angry formation of yellowjackets.

"Then she called me," Harley said. "I drove over there and found her sound asleep under an apple tree, the hammer back on a live round. I unloaded the pump gun, called the sheriff in Boulder, and sat down with her to wait." Harley looked at my eye for a long time, folded his hands on his lap, and worked his lips above his trembling chin. "I thought she was *dead*," he said finally.

I took a few sticks from the woodbox and stirred the fire

alive. Harley hung his coat on a peg beside the door and faced me over the Windsor heater. "So Amy goes to Boulder with a deputy like she's under arrest, and I drag ass home to find *you* all beat up. Would you mind telling me what's going on around here?"

"I took on a load last night. Ended up tangling with that old boy who fenced the water hole. Came out about even."

"He must look pretty bad if it came out even," Harley said bitterly.

"He was on the ground when I left."

"I told you I didn't want to start anything with those people."

I thought of the animals Annie and I had found, of the fight at the dredge pond, of Ted's map, and the dozer cutting its way up Harris Hill. "I *didn't* start it, Harley, I've been trying to leave ever since I got here."

Harley put his hands inside the bib of his overalls. "That's not going to help Amy any."

"I'll go get her, if you want."

"Need to find Annie. She's out running around. You'd think she'd get over that horsing pretty soon, but no! I just don't understand what the hell is happening any more. And I don't like it either!"

I looked outside. Snowflakes the size of silver dollars floated down in the yard. "It's just a change in the weather, Harley. Might as well blame it on the moon."

It snowed, timidly at first, a dreamy curtain of soft pellets that frosted the cattle's shoulders and slowly hid the imperfections of the land. During the evening of the second day, the wind swung around from the north, lifting snow from the ridges and firing it like shot across the flats to drift along the treelines.

I walked the three miles of fence surrounding the hayfields

on the bluff south of the house and turned the cattle loose to forage as best they could. After the first snowfall I put my Ford truck on blocks in the wood yard and took the battery and tires to the cellar. As I was leveling a spot in some soft rock which had crumbled from one wall, I noticed the neck of a mason jug hidden in the dirt. I dug it out and brushed off the grit. Evidently the cork had rotted away, and the whiskey that Harley'd forgotten he'd stashed had evaporated like a dream.

27

I had to admit, he looked pretty sharp. Although he'd probably purchased the western suit and wool topcoat when Truman was president, they were clean, well pressed, and from lack of wear like new. So was the LBJ-model pearl Stetson he held on his lap as I drove toward Montana City.

At the new limerock quarry, Harley lifted a hand. "Pull over here a minute. Let's watch this."

An air-track drill, tall as a barn, bored into the gray stone on the uppermost terrace. Gray dust spewed from the stone and floated east to settle on even grayer snow. To one side of the drill, a mammoth wheel-loader scooped broken rock into semi-type dump trucks, which hauled it away to the Kaiser plant down the canyon. The hill—which I could only vaguely remember, although it had been there when I came in September—had been leveled; from now on, the cutters would be going down, out of sight into the earth. New roads wandered to fuel tanks and shops. The stiff husks of knapweed clung wherever enough dirt remained to anchor them.

Harley shook his head and I put the truck in motion. Below the diggings, two more new roads cut through the hills, one running north and one south toward Flavven's. At the one to the south, a four-by-eight sign said: WELCOME TO HIGH PRAIRIE ESTATES. Harley read the sign out loud but said no more.

I turned north on the Interstate and headed for Helena. Snowplows had swept away the fresh snow, but the asphalt was glassy with ice. Harley held himself erect as he watched the bleak landscape and settlements of new homesites pass by. He would cough, wipe his eyes, and return his attention to the land. Once he pointed at four dogs cavorting in the snow. Again he said nothing.

Uptown, I double-parked at the Power Block and got out, intending to help him cross the slick sidewalk. He waved me back, but I walked with him to the front door anyway.

"This will take awhile. Go ahead and get your hay. Be back here by, say, three o'clock."

"All right, Harley. Do you need anything else?"

"Yeah," he said. "Stop by the vet's and get me a new set of lungs." Harley squared the Stetson on his head, shot his cuffs, struggled with the massive, brass-handled door, and disappeared into the dim marble hallway beyond.

I let the pickup idle as I dragged the bales from the stack, its exhaust rising straight in the icy sky. The team of Belgians that a neighbor had hauled down from the mountains for Smoke stood outside the stack fence, watching the fragrant hay with heavy eyes. Smoke hobbled about on a cane while I worked, an enormous buckle overshoe protecting his cast-laden foot. He petted the draft horses, speaking to them in their own tongue. When I had thirty bales, I roped the corners and put my hook inside the cab. Smoke walked to the truck, swinging the leg like a length of dead wood. He removed his gloves and wrestled his snuff can from an inside shirt. I noticed that the knuckles on his right hand were raw and bruised.

"So how'd that happen?" I asked, pointing to the hand.

Smoke looked up from under bushy eyebrows, a silly, caught-in-the-act look on his face. He shrugged.

"Aw, come on," I said, thinking he'd slipped on the ice around his buildings and taken a header.

"Well," he said shyly, "this is elk season, right?" He thumped the cast with his cane. "So here I am with a busted leg. The more I thought about it, the madder I got. So the other day I drove up to the airport and waited for them chopper jockeys. Sure enough, couple hours before dusk, here they come. When the pilots got to the gate, I told them who I was and why I was there. Then I popped the first one right on the beak."

"Oh balls, Smoke! That make you feel better?"

"You know, it did. And when the guy got up, he said he was sorry as hell, that both him and his partner had felt bad about what had happened and even filed a report with their company." Smoke smiled with satisfaction. "Guy asked me if I'd ever ridden in a helicopter. I told him no, I never had. He asked me if I'd like to, and I said sure. So he turns right around, this guy I'd just dropped, and takes me for a ride. Flew right over Casey Peak. Saw some elk too."

I stared at my father and stamped my feet, trying to keep them warm.

"It turned out pretty good, I have to admit. I really don't think they had time to miss us, trailing that cable and all. After talking with them awhile, I could see they hadn't meant any harm."

"They finding any oil?"

"Way they explained it, nobody will tell them anything. But they did say there would be drilling crews, most likely, working up there in a few months. Say, I heard about your little fracas at the Modern West the other night. Sounded like a pretty good scrap."

"That depended on whose corner you were in."

Smoke grinned his famous grin. "You go right to the top when you pick a fight, don't you? Know who that yardbird is?"

I shook my head and noticed a covey of Hungarian Partridges scurrying across the field toward an overgrown ditch bank.

"That was the youngest Tanners, Steve. Sandy said she stopped in for a shooter or two and he asked her to dance. Next thing she knows you're making kindling out of the furniture with him."

The blue country wavered above the truck's hood. Sky, mountains, snow, shimmering blue and white. Smoke looked toward the mountains, and, I guessed, his elk.

"Harley's not doing well at all, Smoke. I took him to town this morning; it's all he can do to pack his overcoat around."

"Into town for what? Doctor?"

"Lawyer. He didn't say much about it."

"Well, just keep doing what you've been doing. Little things. You know, keep him warm and comfortable, do what he asks, whether it makes sense or not."

The Huns crossed the ditch and scurried on toward another. "Sandy told you about the fight, huh?"

"Yeah. She said, 'When that guy cuts in on a dance, he really cuts in.'" Smoke hit the cast again with his cane. "I sure get a kick out of her," he said and looked away.

"Do you think there's any chance of me getting out of here?"

"Jack," Smoke said and pointed his cane north toward the Belts. "You leave any time you want. Just let me know in advance. I hired that kid again to load hay for me and help me drive. Got orders for a couple hundred ton down along the Powder River already. I'll be on the road off and on, so just let me know ahead of time."

As I drove through East Helena, a furnace crew from the smelter poured a pot of molten dross over the side of the slag heap. They stood against the skyline on their metallic mountain like ancient defenders of an ugly hilltop fort, men of fire and iron, Druids in furnace leathers. Young Arthur and the Von Trash Family Singers would have loved them.

At the A&W, I ordered a couple cheeseburgers and four large vanilla shakes. The carhop wore a blue air force parka over her orange and black uniform. The parka was dabbed with splotches of color, as if it had once belonged to a shaky house painter. I'd never had much luck with carhops, as I imagined most teenagers did, but I had ridden my BSA Goldstar from burger joint to burger joint on that nameless Friday-night quest, leaking oil in parking lots all over town only to ride away alone into the neon sunset. High school in Helena had been a torture. The sons and daughters of state government officials, doctors, lawyers, and dentists had divided the school into castes with themselves, their parents' money, and their fathers' cars on top. The best looking of those girls took Latin. I was the worst Latin student in school, but I hung right in there. And the Goldstar—I'd sold that to pay my rodeo fees when I dropped out of college.

The IGA was crowded. Women, who as girls had survived the German camps only to marry displaced smelter workers and become alcoholic grandmothers, charged their shopping carts down the aisles, the frenzy of food bright as frost in their craving eyes. Their husbands and sons on afternoon shift gagged on lead smoke above the furnaces, probably dreaming cold beers and peace at home. I wheeled my cart along, picking up fresh vegetables, whole-wheat rolls, yogurt, and ice cream, foods I hoped would do Harley some good. I picked up a few magazines for myself and noticed a book on the paperback shelf by Duncan Carlisle. *The Wrong Ace*. Guy on the cover wearing a shoulder holster and holding a whiskey neat. I thumbed through it as I waited in the checkout line. When I looked up, I saw Sandy Martinez clearing the door beside a tall man in a western-cut leather jacket and cowboy hat covered with feathers. It wasn't hard, even from his back, to tell who it was.

28

The cast iron grates in the Monarch range clinked as they cooled. Harley napped in his recliner, his ashen face reflecting the flickering images of the TV. He slept there now most of each night, saying it was closer to the stove and easier to breathe sitting up. The times when I'd mentioned having a doctor come out or spoke of getting a prescription for his cough, Harley had simply switched the subject, acting like he hadn't heard.

"Dear Jack." The card showed a young cowboy sprawled in the front seat of a high-finned Caddy convertible, his feet up on one door. An oil rig, strung with lights like a Christmas tree, winked in the background. The cowboy held a beer in one hand and you could tell he owned the rig. He had that kind of smile. "I'm going to interview for jobs in Victoria after Christmas. I need to get on, and I think it's a good way to start. I'll send an address if I decide to stay. Wish you could be here during the holidays—we're having a Christmas goose."

It was signed with an X.

Harley rustled in his chair, coughed himself awake, and got stiffly to his feet. "The fire's down," he said.

I crinkled some newspaper and stuffed it onto the dull coals in the range, then added some fine-chopped pitch pine and two small chunks of split wood.

"Dozed off," Harley muttered, clearing his throat. "And I had the darnedest dream." He hugged himself, gazing up at the ax marks in the beams overhead, coming back slowly from where he'd been in his sleep. "I dreamed," he said and snuffled, "that I was mucking out a drift down on the number-three level in the Veracruz, just like when I worked there as a kid. Only, funny thing was, you were with me and we were shoveling mud, see, when one of the drillers hollers back, 'Fire in the hole!'"

Harley drew a handkerchief from his overalls and wiped at his nose. "Powder monkey shoots the charge down at the end of the drift, and you and I take our shovels and go down to see what needs to be done next. But, see, the whole end of the tunnel was lit up bright as day, like they'd blasted right out into the sky!" Harley shook his head. "The number-three level was down two hundred feet!"

I struck a match to the newspaper and listened to the fire whump up the stovepipe.

"Worst job I ever had," Harley said. "Cold, muddy, dripping son of a bitch." He stepped up to the stove and held out his hands. I rattled the grates clean and opened the draft. "Never do it again . . . no matter what they paid. Back then I made fifty cents a shift." He sighed. "Four bits! For eight or ten hours working bent over in a slicker, shoveling mud in the damned dark."

I didn't say anything. Watching him as he talked, I saw the boy he'd once been flicker alive and die.

Harley noticed my face. Abruptly, he shifted subjects. "Listen here, if you need something to do with yourself," he said, "that upper meadow needs a lot of work. Get in there, cut the brush and trees, and burn the trash. Way it is now, you can't even see the creek in places."

"Sure thing," I answered. It was one of those indefinite jobs that came to mind on winter evenings—one that might someday get done or not. "You bet, Harley."

"No rush, you've got all the time in the world."

I closed the damper on the stovepipe. "Whatever happened to that roan you won at Montana City?" I asked.

"Oh, had him around here for years. Got to be a regular pest, spoiled, you know. He got old. Dropped dead in front of the hay barn. Why?"

"I just got to thinking about him is all."

"Hummph. You been sleeping under his worthless hide upstairs for twenty-some years," Harley said. "It was a cold morning, the day he keeled over, so I just skinned him out right where he fell."

Harley took the last of his milk shakes from the refrigerator. "Boy, these hit the spot," he said and returned to the never-ending life of television.

I studied the coals glowing through the open grid in the draft. My eyebrow itched where the stitches had held the skin. I wondered how long Harley'd last, how long it would be before winter made up its mind, how long before Smoke picked up Sandy Martinez's ever-winding trail.

I rested on the weight bench between sets, looking at the yellow pages scattered on the writing table. They reflected the soft yellow light of the kerosene lamp and my lack of resolve. I didn't know what to say except that I was sorry, and I was tired of saying that.

Tires squealed on the frozen snow in the yard. I looked out the dormer window and saw Smoke climb from his truck. He pulled his elk rifle from the dashboard, his cane from the front seat, and limped around to the passenger-side door.

I toweled off my neck and face, pulled on an extra sweat shirt, and went downstairs to see what he was up to now. Harley turned down the TV, and slowly, careful of his balance, stepped into his buckle overshoes.

Smoke limped through the door, carrying the bolt-action Model 70 Winchester in the crook of one arm. With his other hand he lifted a bloody clover-seed sack, heavy with heart and liver. "Got my bull and fell on my ass," he said, handing me the dripping sack of meat. He shifted his weight to the cane and held up the rifle. He'd broken the sling and shattered the rear lens in the WWII vintage scope.

"How many points, June?" Harley asked, seeming to forget that Smoke had a cast on one leg.

"Six on one side, seven on the other. I didn't get him out, Dad."

"Oh?" Harley seemed disappointed, then seeing as he already had his galoshes on, he stepped outside to urinate in the dark. I washed the heart and liver and the seamless cloth sack as Smoke scrubbed his bloody hands beside me at the sink.

"I'm going to need some help. He's in a bad spot."

"Crystal?"

"Higher up, on the Henry Creek side."

I shook my head, felt a smile spreading across my face. "How'd you get up *there?*"

"I just took my time. I've been hunting lower, but the elk aren't moving yet. Too mild." Smoke dried his hands and forearms with a rough towel. "Just couldn't seem to tip him over. Put three of those softpoints through him, and all the time he was plowing further into the doghair. Clear day like today, they probably heard that ought-six clear to the men's room in the Clancy Bar."

It was then that I realized hunting season was over. Harley lit the lamp, and we sat down together at the kitchen table. Smoke removed the broken sling from his rifle, punched new holes in the worn leather, and laced the joined pieces together. His hands trembled as he worked, the exhaustion of his day with the elk plain upon his face. He unscrewed the broken scope and bore-sighted the factory buckhorn on a knothole in the log parlor wall. The rifle looked like it had been dragged a good distance behind a runaway pack string: the stock was gouged and scratched, the bluing burned off barrel and bolt.

Harley watched Smoke as he worked, his eyes alive and

intent. "My old dad would have got a big charge out of *you,*
June," he said to my father. "He was the best wing shot in
this damn country."

"I didn't know that," I said. "I didn't think he was much
of a hunter."

"Ha!" Harley said. "He was a gamekeeper in Devonshire
before we came to this country. Loved to shoot. Should have
seen him. This country was alive with birds when we got
here."

"Why'd your folks leave England?"

"Because of me. My lungs. Had consumption so bad
when I was small they laid me out for dead once. Doctor
came late in the night and I was still *alive!* Doctor told my
dad, 'You take him to a dry climate, or you'll bury him,' so
here we come. Cheated 'em out of eighty-three more years
too, by God!"

Smoke looked up, catching Harley's slip, and winked at
me without changing expression.

I watched them and listened, and it seemed nothing had
changed over the years, that I was small again, absorbed in
the doings of grown men: the same table, the same soft light,
the same voices. All that was missing was Summer's confident laugh.

Smoke poured a pan full of warm water, added some Ep-
som salts, and unbuckled his overshoe. He unwrapped some
rags and exposed his foot. The big toe below the cast looked
like a hammer-smashed thumb, the nail purple and black,
the flesh bruised and bloody. He had cut away most of the
cast around his foot and hacksawed off the part above his
knee. He noticed me staring and said, "It's pretty steep up
there." He winked at Harley and settled his foot in the water
and closed his eyes. "You remember that time I got out of
the hospital and killed a buck the same afternoon, cast and
all?" he asked Harley.

"Got him horseback, didn't you?"

"Uh-huh. Must be getting old." He opened his eyes and

looked at me. "Better hit the hay, kid. We'll be out of here early."

I glanced back at them as I climbed the stairs, and the feeling of having stepped into an exact moment of the past returned once more. I didn't know it would be the last time we'd sit like that together in the night. They spoke in low voices at the table, and I couldn't make out their words.

The horsehide robe on my bunk smelled of tanning agents and dust. As I lay warming toward sleep, I remembered how Smoke had long ago come in the night, lifted me from bed, and carried me into the truck lights at the open machine-shop door. Our breath rose through frost crystals in little clouds, and if I laid my head back on his shoulder, I could see the falling frost sliced by slivers of light pouring from cracks in the board-and-batten gables.

I remembered shivering. Not just cold sending those out-of-control vibrations through my body, but the musky smell of Smoke's mackinaw, the rank odors of elk urine and sweat, woodsmoke and blood, and the bite of rifle-bore cleaner, cutting the rest like gall. It was a blend of smells, a scent all its own, which I would remember as the essence of the man who was my father.

We'd look without speaking at the bull, his hind legs split at the hocks, spitted over the iron knobs of a hardwood singletree. The singletree hung by a clevis from the chain hoist that ran up to the rough-cut four-by-eight roof beams.

Year after year the bulls hung there, their noses touching pools of slick blood, puddled black and greasy on the cement floor, their heads twisted at wrong angles by the arching weight of their antlers. At first he had just carried me out and let me look. As I got bigger, he'd sometimes say something about how it had been, something like, "Lucky shot. Took him on a dead run at the upper end of Montgomery Park."

I didn't realize dream had overtaken memory until he shook me awake. "Time to roll," Smoke said, and limped quietly down the hall, careful of the cast, so as not to wake Harley.

29

I stopped Smoke's truck in a dark thicket of young spruce and killed the engine. Wind tormented the trees and rocked the pickup. The unnamed canyon drained northwest from the upper Elkhorns, steep and dark and seldom hunted. During season, Jeepers would take a look down from the ridge road and decide to head on toward easier country lower on the mountain.

"Let's just wait a bit," Smoke said, pouring himself a steaming cup of thermos coffee. He had dressed in Malone pants and wool shirts, and a hooded white jacket he'd sewn from a bedsheet.

"What's Harley up to with the lawyer?" I asked.

"He's tightening up some loose ends." Smoke rolled his frosted window down and spit his cud of tobacco into the snow. "Title verifications, updating some records so he can make out a will. You know, one section of that summer pasture is still in my mom's name."

"Jesus, Smoke. She's been dead forty years."

"Forty-four." He shook his head. "Just something he never got around to changing." He rummaged in his canvas pack, making sure he had his meat saw, Gerber stone, nylon rope, and sandwiches. "That deal of Amy's got him thinking, I guess."

Off south, the Tyzer Peaks took white shape against the various layers of gray sky. The sky bore down upon the hills, upon us. It wasn't any wonder the old-time homesteaders had gone crazy. Fifteen hours of night, nine hours of smudged grays and nothing to live for but work. When Harley was young, madness and suicide had been wholesale among the isolated settlers, a way out when you couldn't go back home.

"If that chunk of summer pasture was fenced it would almost make a ranch out of Harley's place," Smoke said. "Over two square miles out there, most of it good north-slope grass."

"Dream on, Smoke. You told me yourself that guy on the Harris place couldn't get water—Harley's land must be five or six hundred feet above him. Cows won't travel that far every day anyway, not clear to Jackson Creek, for a drink. You know that."

Smoke shrugged. "Water's the hang-up, all right. No argument there. It's all limerock, too, till you get to the Veracruz."

"I've got to haul those strays to Butte pretty soon. Another six inches of snow, I'll be buying hay. No future in that. Mind if I use your stock truck?"

"You've got a nice little bunch of cows. The calves aren't much, but those big cows are the kind that make you money."

"Most of those old sisters only have a couple calves left in 'em. I'd better get rid of them before they start going gaunt on me."

Smoke spoke slowly, carefully. "Listen, Jack. You've been doing real fine since you've been back. If you want to keep them awhile, I'll front you the hay. Why don't you just hang in there?"

I pulled my Scotch cap low over my eyes. "That's what the orderlies used to say at Fitzsimmons. We had a thirty-six-year-old PFC on my ward named Slate. Slate the Sleeper, everybody called him. He would nod off walking down stairs or at a drinking fountain or during a meal. He was always falling asleep and falling down. 'Hang in there,

Slate the Sleeper,' the orderlies used to say, 'better keep movin' or you'll turn to stone.'

"He hung in there, too. One morning they found him hanging from a steam pipe in the latrine, a bedsheet around his neck and his tongue swollen the color of eggplant. He'd pinned a note to himself. It said: 'Wake me up *now,* you motherfuckers.'"

Smoke scratched at the frost on the window with his fingernail. "It takes time. We all had to heal up when we came home. Harley, me, now you. But at least we got a chance to get better, to live."

I shook my head. Since I'd come home I had gained strength with each passing day, but Smoke and Harley, it seemed, had declined as my strength grew.

"Let's get that bull," I said and pulled on my gloves.

Outside, I spread a white tarp over the truck and weighted it with small logs and spruce boughs, then shouldered Smoke's pack and followed him to the lip of the canyon. In minutes the wind would erase our trail, as it had covered the tracks of the truck. We entered the jack pine and started down.

Within a hundred yards we were sliding into trees, hanging onto limbs to brake our next step. Under the foot or so of snow, slide rock covered with ice clattered and wobbled as we shifted our feet. The wind dropped in the timber, and finally we came to the spot where Smoke had jumped the bull the day before. Blood and hair from the first shot were still visible under a skiff of spindrift. Bark had exploded from a tree a few yards away. When Smoke noticed me looking at the tree, he said, "I hit him in the neck. Never touched bone at all."

My knees began to shake from the strain of standing. My feet crowded the front of my rubber boots, and I understood how Smoke had mashed his toes the day before. A couple hundred yards farther, more blood and hair. This time the bull had gone down, wallowed, slid, and come up running, heading back uphill through deadfall that would have stopped a good horse. "You're tough when you can take that," Smoke said, pointing at the marks in the snow. He loved the elk with a primitive love, for their wild intelligence, for their beauty, and for what they could stand.

The bull had plowed into a thicket of baby fir before the third shot broke his neck. During the night he'd frozen stiff. I cut off the head and all four legs at the knee, then stood the carcass on the stumps of the legs, cut the hide along the backbone from head to tail, and began to saw lengthwise through the spine. I was overheated and felt awkward; the saw refused to cut straight, and the harder I worked, the farther off center I cut. My hands and boots were covered with gore. As the meat separated above the shoulders, I saw splinters of the copper-jacketed bullet resting against the bone. *Garrett has them back at the gun when the tires hit the ground, leveling the bubbles, adjusting back to the red-and-white aiming stakes, spinning in fuses, packing powder bags into canisters, slamming rounds into the tube, and jumping back, beyond the deadly reach of recoil . . . Garrett pushing, hounding, harassing them without mercy . . .*

"Let me spell you," Smoke said, laying his hand on my shoulder. "Take it easy. Take a break."

I got out of his way so he could straddle the bull, and with short clean strokes, pacing himself and pausing now and then to rest, he reduced the animal to halves. I was surprised at the steadiness of Smoke's strength. An old bull himself, he carried himself and his cast with dignity.

I cut each side in two, just behind the shortribs. As I started up the wooded slope, pulling a heavy front quarter on a length of nylon rope, a fine snow began to fall.

After my third trip up the hill, Smoke took some sandwiches and Mars Bars from his pack. We ate, watching the thickening snow. It seemed a good time to try to say what had been on my mind all along. "I will stay at the ranch, until Harley dies," I said.

"You figure Harley doesn't know that?"

"I just wanted you to know."

"All right, I know. Thanks."

"So if you need to haul hay, go ahead. Maybe spell me between trips."

"Fine. Let's get that haunch and get out of here."

I worked my way around boulders and through snow-brush, panting and scrambling and pulling. Smoke went on ahead, favoring the leg, but gaining on me steadily until he stopped to rest. As I was about to go around him with the hind quarter, he touched my arm. He pointed his nose into the wind like a hound, taking quick little breaths. All I could smell was the day-old kill and myself. But on the wind, he had caught the odor of elk. And on the wind above us came the low moan of an engine.

The Cessna broke over the ridge above us, flying at stall speed, gliding down the canyon, working the wind like a hawk. "Look at your boots," Smoke said, "not the plane."

The skid trail behind us was three feet wide and a foot deep, speckled here and there with flecks of blood. Smoke tried to hold his breath and giggled. "Fish and Fucking Game," he said, "those silly bastards."

"They can see where we've dragged him," I said.

"On a clear day, maybe. But they didn't even see the elk they spooked out."

The plane turned and added power, climbing through the curtain of falling snow toward the other side of the canyon. And the elk, somewhere above us, moved off without a sound.

30

Harley seemed to get taller as he lost weight. He didn't want much company, so I spent my days outside, rebuilding worn sets of tire chains, dragging bales to my white-backed cattle, and taking long, late-afternoon walks on Smoke's snowshoes. The storm that caught us as we drove home with the elk lasted. Winter came down from the mountains as if it had come to stay.

I turned the roan out to the fenced Homestead pasture, between the barn and the Veracruz, where he could graze on the wind-cleared ridges. He trotted away with his head high; free again, he humped his back and bucked a few jumps, then ambled back to the gate and hung his head over the top wire, question marks in his eyes. I gave him a linty sugar lump from my coat pocket and scratched his frosty chin. "You'll figure it out, my friend," I told him, and he did. By the time I'd hiked back to the house, he was gone.

I shoveled paths to the outhouse, the pitch-wood pile, the shop, and even to the milk house, where we sometimes hung fresh meat. A small, chaletlike building, it had been built with whiskey money for processing milk and butter and cream. After Harley had married, milk gradually replaced moonshine in the cream cans he took to town in the back of his Model A, and dairying moved from a sideline cover to a full-time family occupation. My grandmother had run the processing end of the milk business, and the milk house had been hers. When she died, the dairying staggered to a halt.

Harley traded their milk cows for Herefords, most of his workhorses for iron-wheeled tractors, two-bottomed plows, and grain drills.

Her churns, butter molds, cream separator, and iceboxes stood where she had left them. But instead of the bare concrete floor I remembered, I found, piled from one wall to the other, hundreds—at a glance, well over a thousand—brand-new steel fence posts, still banded in bundles of five and stacked carefully to save space. Behind the posts, piled six high from wall to wall, stood four shiny rows of rolled barbed wire. To one side, fifty-pound boxes of staples rested on bundles of twist-on wire fence staves. Except for corner posts, there was enough material to fence half the ranch.

I backed out the door and bumped into Harley. He had been standing behind me, watching; even wrapped in his belted coat, he looked miserably cold. He'd had the heart for something his lungs wouldn't let him do.

"I'll draw you a map of the corner stones out there," he said. "Then all you'll have to do is have a surveyor connect them."

"Come on," I said. "Let's go warm up."

Inside, I pulled my tobacco pouch and papers from my shirt, opened the lid on the Windsor stove, and dropped them in. Harley sat at the table and, with a carpenter's pencil, diagramed the north half of the place, the unfenced land. He placed an X at each spot where he knew a stone still stood. And he explained the lay of the land near each spot so I could find them. When he finished, he rolled up the butcher-paper map and handed it to me. "Be sure your dad sees that too," he said.

"Would you mind if I borrowed your Krag?"

Harley went to the kitchen and pulled the rifle from behind the dish cupboard. "You might as well have it," he said, snapping the bolt open. Crude by today's standards, the .30–40 Krag had been standard infantry issue during the

Spanish-American War. "Don't hock that," he said, and
handed me the weapon.

A light gust of wind rattled loose panes of glass in the
kitchen windows. Our eyes met, his gray and clear.

"No, sir. I won't," I answered.

Snow had drifted above the third wire of the old four-wire
fence, carved and corniced into girlish lines where curlicues
spilled off the high ground. I hiked north past the timbered
gallus frame on the Veracruz and the Homestead wire to
the unfenced land. My snowshoes squeaked on the wind-
slabbed drifts, the tails whispering behind me as I stepped
ahead. The late sun peaked through wind-torn shards of
cloud, lighting the high prairie gold and white, the fir fence
posts a deep, deep red, and the snow a radiant, shimmering
blue. It seemed odd to be here in the winter and not be
working full time with Harley and Summer on cattle, not to
be out on foot checking cows, carrying in bum calves, and
loading hay each morning for two hundred head. There
were times in the winter, if you kept to a strict routine, when
the ranch seemed to run itself. Then something happened: a
heifer would fall on the ice and break her pelvis; a young
bull would lose his footing and end wedged on his back in
the creek; a cow would have a stillborn calf, which, after
hours of agonized, frenzied labor, you pulled out in pieces.

Sometimes you lost the cow and saved the calf. I'd raised
one of those orphans once. His legs had been stretched by
the force of the calf-puller, his hips dislocated. I named him
Shorty McLeod, because at first he was such a runt. Shorty's
front knees looked like softballs, his back legs were stiff as
stilts. On separate occasions he almost died of scours, pneumonia, and grain bloat. For years he tagged along after me,
even when he weighed as much as Harley's bulls. One Tues-
day, while I was in school, old Shorty went to Butte with a
truckload of canners, still thinking he was a bucket calf.

It was that one thing, the cow down or the stillborn calf, that put you behind on an already tight schedule, when, if you were calving hard, you threw a canvas over the hay bunk in the barn and slept in your bloody coveralls, because in two hours you'd be back outside with a flashlight. And that went on, seven days a week, until the weather broke or you did. Now the cattle and Summer were gone, and as I moped around trying to find excuses for being outside, I couldn't help missing them both.

From a bare hill Smoke called the Lone Tree, I could make out the new road snaking up Harris Hill. When the Chinook winds came in February, their sudden warmth would draw frost from the ground overnight and the road would become a river of mud. I hiked on north until I reached another rise in the land. Almost on top, just as Harley had said, stood a stone with an X and ¼ carved on its face. I turned east and tried to imagine where the fence line would have run, what the country would look like with the bright wire stretching across it.

Off west, I noticed smoke rising from Amy's house, a slender wisp that bent and rode away on the wind. The men in the station wagon had turned out to be realtors hired to appraise Amy's property. They hadn't been told about folks living there, or so they claimed, and maybe because they wouldn't disclose their employers, they declined to file charges. Annie brought Amy home, and the old lady acted—or so Annie had told me later—like the Joan of Arc of Casey Creek.

I retraced my steps, gliding along on the snowshoes until I again stood at the Lone Tree. It was where Smoke had earned his name. In the early '20s, Harley was involved in a fence dispute with a neighbor named Saint 'Amour. Saint 'Amour claimed Harley's fence was off the line and when Harley refused to move it, the Frenchman set three fires in an attempt to burn him out. Harley had loaded as much of the household goods as he could into wagons and took

Smoke along to guard the stuff. Harley left him at the Lone Tree with a .30–30 and told him to direct firefighters and not let anybody near the wagons. One crusty old man named Hirsch had ridden up later, and my father, who was only six years old and scared, had simply pointed toward the distant fire and said, "Smoke." That had tickled old Hirsch, who was probably drunk at the time, and he called the boy Smoke from then on.

A light aircraft cleared Harris Hill, but just before it passed, it throttled back and turned, carving a tight circle above me. It was the Fish and Game Cessna. I waved the rifle like a Kurdish tribesman and did a little dance on the snowshoes.

"We're coming for your wives and children tonight!" I shouted and beat my chest with my free hand. The pilot probably thought I was crazy. He added power and turned abruptly away.

Sheep Mountain stood hooded by bruise-colored clouds, stark against the light where I stood and the higher, wind-combed clouds off south. As I looked at the mountain, I heard them, high above me, almost out of sight. The last ragged flights of migrating northern geese. I watched them struggle on south, the vee stretching and reforming until they were out of sight, and I wondered why Smoke called the hill the Lone Tree. There wasn't any tree, no stump, or even a scattering of roots or broken limbs. There was nothing at the Lone Tree but rock and grass and wind.

IV

31

"And if I'm not there in an hour, you come help me dig out," Annie said on the telephone.

Harley didn't feel up to company, so he climbed the stairs to his room, opened the floor vents above the stove, and closed his door. He and I had settled into a solitude broken only by Smoke's occasional visits, when he brought groceries, grain, and hay between his twice-weekly trips to eastern Montana. During the days, I kept the stoves going, fed my cattle, cooked meals that Harley most often ignored, and packed a bucket of oats out to the roan each afternoon. At night, I pumped iron. I'd gained fifteen pounds in less than four months; during my solitary afternoon hikes on snowshoes, I rediscovered parts of the place I'd almost forgotten. The creek became gorged with ice, drifts grew hard beneath a freezing wind, and the road to town became a trial. Harley hung on; one day bled into another, and I dreamed an early spring.

I put on my insulated coveralls and went into the yard to wait for Annie. Snow sparkled in the soft light of the windows and squeaked under my boots. I looked into the heavens; the stars seemed as close as the frost falling above me. In the stillness, I could hear the gentle movements of the cattle in the shelter shed and the distant gnashing of machinery at the new quarry.

The little Jeep rounded a bend at the red gate, its lights sweeping across eighteen inches of crusted snow in the fields. When Annie pulled into the yard and killed her lights, I opened the plywood door on the Jeep and helped her out. She reached into the vehicle for a large, red-wrapped box. "Ho, ho, *ho,*" Annie said, making her voice go low and husky. "Merry Christmas, little boy!"

In the light of the Aladdin in the kitchen, she looked like a large-breasted Santa, dressed in red coveralls and a red stocking hat. I put my finger to my lips and pointed at the ceiling. Annie nodded and handed me the box. "Open it," she whispered. "It's Christmas Eve!"

I put the box on the oak table and folded back the wrapping paper. Inside, I found foil-wrapped paper plates of homemade cookies, fudge, and Harley's favorite, Amy's divinity. Below the cookies and candy lay a bottle of Remy Martin cognac and some newspaper-covered Christmas-tree decorations. I couldn't help but smile. "For Christ's sake, Annie—"

She stood on her toes and quickly kissed me. "Got you," she said, and I saw that she had been holding a sprig of mistletoe behind my back and above my head. She looked around the kitchen and parlor. "What? No tree? A thousand acres of timber and *no* Christmas tree?" She pulled up the hood on her blazing coveralls and drew it tight around her beaming face. She took my hand and said, "Come on, Scooter. Let's go get you one!"

I found a length of light rope and a small Hudson Bay ax in the shop. Together we trudged across the frozen creek and up the rise toward the hay fields south of the house. With the stars and quarter moon and snow, we had enough light, even in the darker stands of timber, to see each other clearly.

"So you forgot all about Christmas. That's a real bad sign."

"I've had my hands full with Harley."

"I know. Why are we still whispering?"

We laughed, but even our laughter seemed hushed as we

entered the first of the glittering fields. We plowed along, listening to the snow whispering under our boots and looking wide-eyed at the glittering winter landscape around us. The drifted snow in the open would hold us up for a few steps, then we'd fall through to our knees. Finally, we stopped to rest. Below us, toward Saint 'Amour's, several small engines whined and growled in the night. They seemed to draw nearer, then fade away.

"Snowmobiles?" Annie asked, pushing her hood back. I shrugged and started on again, toward the far edge of the field. Annie puffed up beside me and took my gloved hand in hers. "Saw your buddies in town the other night," she said. "The ones who were with you at the Modern West."

"Hum?"

"Boy, were they on a tear. One of them had sold something to the movies. The midget said to be sure and goose Little Orris. That's you? Saw Smokey's girlfriend too. She was with that guy you clobbered. He looks real nice with his nose spread across his face like a gob of Silly Putty."

"Trouble with a capital T."

"Which?"

"Both."

"Well, as long as Smoke doesn't find out—" Annie let the idea drift.

"I wonder sometimes if maybe he already has," I said. "He's pretty close when it comes to her."

We entered the thicket of little trees, feeling the cold-sharpened needles on our faces as we brushed through them. Annie picked one and I bent to cut away the lower limbs. Again we heard the wrapped-tight buzzing of two-cycle engines. They seemed to be coming right toward us from the south.

I cut the bushy fir and tied the rope to its slender trunk. As we stepped into the open, several mule deer bounded past, moving as fast as they could in the crusted snow. Lights appeared, wavering through the trees below us, and suddenly there they were, four snowmobiles, chasing each other and the lunging animals through the drifts in Harley's field.

"Hey!" Annie shouted, waving the ax. "Hey, goddamn you!" They didn't see us, and couldn't hear Annie as they slalomed past at forty miles an hour.

I grabbed her arm. "Forget it," I said. "Let it go."

She jerked her arm away. "You're just like Harley! Give and give until they're walking all over you!"

"What the hell should I do? Get mad, raise hell with every dumb-ass that wanders across the place. Give me a break!"

"They had to cut a fence somewhere to get in here, didn't they?"

"Let them crash and die. Who cares?"

Annie pulled back her hood and said, as if we'd just met for a fight, "That's the one thing I don't like about you." She looked north, toward the snowy mirage of hills beyond the creek, and said, "Ted's thinking of selling, you know."

"Horseshit."

"Yes he is. Wait till you have a trailer park right up the creek from you."

"Not Ted."

"Well, you can't blame him. It's tougher every year to run in the black; he doesn't have any retirement plan to count on; his boys will probably leave home. What's he going to do when he's too old to work?"

"None of that's new in this country."

"Right. And nobody ever came around talking six figures before either." Annie's face was drawn with anger. "Is that what you'd do? Sell out?"

"I won't have to worry about that, Annie. I'm just the chore boy on this outfit. Always have been, always would be."

"You'd better come back to reality pretty soon, Scooter." Annie snatched the tow rope and pulled the tree along behind her. "Before you wake up and find you've lost it all."

"Lost what?" I said, feeling anger rising in me too. "This

rock pile? The privilege of scratching fourteen hours a day for the pure pride of going broke on *this* place?" I took the rope back and pulled the little tree on as if I were towing a whale. "This is not going to be a loss, Annie. I'm sorry about your troubles, but don't get in my face about what I ought or ought not to be doing. If I hadn't promised Summer—"

"This is your home, Scooter . . . you grew up here. Your people are buried here . . . if you hadn't promised Summer what?"

"That I'd keep an eye on the old guys. Until he got back."

"But Scooter, he's not coming back."

"It doesn't matter. I left anyway."

The stars and moon threw our bulky shadows across the quivering snow as if we were prehistoric monsters dragging a kill across a glacier. We plowed along for a while in silence, facing the aurora of light above Helena, which glowed in the sky beyond the Bald Hills. As we entered the pines above the creek, Annie slipped her arm through mine. "Let me help you put up the tree," she said. "We're not having one this year."

32

As I came in from the pitch pile with a coal bucket full of kindling, Harley said, "Sit down here a minute, mister, I want to talk to you."

He had dressed for the first time in several days, putting on his black jeans and a plaid shirt he'd worn through at the elbows. His long johns showed gray under the shirt. I put the kindling beside the kitchen range and sat down, facing him across the hardwood table. His neck and cheeks were scabbed in places where I'd nicked him, trying to help him shave. When he spoke, his voice was strong, but he stopped now often to cough.

"Your dad tell you about the lawyer?"

"No. He didn't mention any particulars."

He nodded and laid one of his great hands on the table. "You know," he said, "I've had enough winter to last me a lifetime."

Although he'd lost maybe half his normal weight, his hands stayed the same: massive, sinuous, and crossed by long hard veins that lately had turned a pale blue. Hands made by work, but also the kind of hands—I'd heard from enough people by then to believe—made to fight.

"Winters," he said. "Since I was your age, I've seen some, I'll tell you. Some hard, like this one looks to be, some so open I could plow in February. But every one takes something out of you." He tried to clear his throat and gagged, bending further over as he coughed, until his head was almost between his knees. I looked away, watching snow spin in whorls against the half-frosted window. After the last few days, I'd look at almost anything rather than watch him cough.

Gradually he got his throat clear, spit into a five-gallon grease can at the foot of the bed I'd arranged for him beside the stove, and breathing hard, he said, "You'll see."

He wiped his mouth and chin with a paper towel. "I come home like you, only to nothing. My folks dead and in the ground. Our stock run off, stuff scattered all over the ranch, no feed. And just about the time I get to where I'm breaking even, I almost got shot by a drunk."

He drummed his fingers on the table. The middle finger was stiff, as it had been most of his life, since he'd stumbled, running a boyhood errand with a jar of mustard gripped in his gloveless hand. He broke his fall with that hand and the bottle had shattered into knives and needles. Now, on the tabletop, that finger hit harder than the rest, making a dull flat snap each time it came down on the polished oak.

"Me and Slicker took the county road contract that year. You know, to keep the snow plowed from the head of Jackson to Montana City. We had wind that winter; you never seen such wind . . . blow all day out of the west, then switch around and tear all night out of the north. We had Slicker's iron-wheeled patrol for a snowplow, and my four teams strung out, up to their cruppers in drifts."

He glanced up from his hand. "We had to go right past Bill Hirsch's place back then, and usually we'd stop to rest the horses and thaw ourselves out. Old Bill lived off there by himself in the rocks, and he drank some. Go in spells, you know, sometimes worse than others. Well, this one morning we stopped, it was almost Christmas. Bill was at the jug. Had been for days. We went on in, stood around the stove and jawed for a while, and Slicker told Bill that if he'd sober up during the day he could ride the plow back with us that night to spend Christmas at Slicker's, you know, have a couple decent meals. Bill said sure, fine; he'd dry out."

His eyes watered from talking and coughing. His skin had turned the color of ashes, and at that moment I saw he was going to die on me. If Harley knew what I was thinking, he didn't let on. Instead, he folded those big hands on his lap and looked past me at the snow coming down outside.

"We had a hell of a time," he said. "Slicker operated the patrol, and I handled the horses. Hitting those drifts was like trying to plow concrete. When the blade jammed, the wheelers and middle teams would lunge to keep up with the leaders, and that old iron-wheeled grader would ride right up the drift and flip over. Got so bad I finally took to riding the left leader to stop 'em when Slicker got pitched off the platform. Even so, we tore hell out of my harness."

I took my cup to the kitchen range. The teakettle had boiled almost dry. I used what water there was to fix a cup of instant coffee.

"It was damn near dusk by the time we got back up to Bill's," he continued. "The horses were done in, we still had Cutler Grade to pull, and there was old Bill, drunker than seven hundred dollars. Slicker told him that we weren't *goin'* to take him, seeing as how we had enough trouble already. Slicker didn't smooth it over none either, and old Bill got mad."

I sipped at the sour coffee, and I waited. Not for him to continue, but for the next fit of coughing; coughing he would last through like a man taking a beating, hanging on like a man who doesn't believe in the end that he can be beat. I began to sweat under my wool shirts. I thought about walking to Clancy for cigarettes.

Harley steadied himself, leaning forward with a hand on each knee. "We got the horses lined out," he said. "But when I seen Bill clear the door with his rifle I bailed off the leader and yelled at Slicker to catch hold of something. I started pounding that lead horse on the ass with my open hand. He was a big, cowy Percheron, and Christ could he pull. Slicker had just lowered the blade and of course it jammed on the first drift we hit. We ran along the offside, hanging onto the hames, clear to the quarry, dragging the patrol on its side. When we stopped and looked back, old Bill was just standing in the door of his shack, holding his thirty-thirty in one hand like he'd forgot it."

Harley rested a minute. The telephone dinged, as it did lately, just before the lines went down. Before he could go on, I stood and took my herder's coat off the nail on the door, and listened to wind rattle the windows; I listened to the telephone that didn't work right, and to my grand-father's breathing.

"Got to get some air," I said.

"Oh?" Harley stood, walked into the log front room to sit beside the stove, and folded his hands. "Poor day," he said. "Too damn much wind."

As I buttoned on my coat, the rattle rose again in his throat and he straightened in the chair to cough. When he caught his breath, I pulled the Krag from behind the cup-board and tucked it under my arm. I had taken to carrying the heavy rifle on the walks I took to look at the place. I hadn't bothered to load it since he'd given it to me, but I knew that if I went without it I'd somehow feel wrong . . . aimless maybe, or unbalanced.

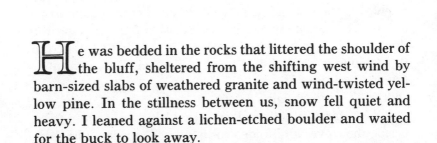

33

He was bedded in the rocks that littered the shoulder of the bluff, sheltered from the shifting west wind by barn-sized slabs of weathered granite and wind-twisted yellow pine. In the stillness between us, snow fell quiet and heavy. I leaned against a lichen-etched boulder and waited for the buck to look away.

Wisps of hemp baler twine, bleached and rotten, hung in trees along the sheltered trail where we had once fed cattle with a team and hay boat. The stock followed us there single file, between where the buck now lay and where I stood. My grandfather drove the team, while Summer and I forked wafers of sweet hay to the trailing cows. He spoke now and then to his horses, and he called his cattle into a trot; I cut the frozen twine, pitched hay, and dreamed leaving. I had dreamed cars and girls, highways that would take me to distant places, rodeo buckles and beer. Each day we'd hung the twine from the bales in a different tree, like dreams hung out to dry. Now that I owned cattle of my own, I thought about feeding them here, when storms roared day after day out of the southwest, tearing themselves open on the Divide, and spilling their strength east. The team we'd fed with had been old by then. Very old and quite steady.

I eased the glove off my right hand. The shell casings in my coat pocket were cold, even against my numb fingers, and so was the rifle bolt as I opened the sloppy Mauser action and thumbed two rounds into the side-mounted magazine tray.

The buck turned his head, pointing his black-tipped ears toward something I couldn't see. I slipped my left arm through the homemade harness-leather sling and brought the barrel slowly up. I knew I wasn't ready; that I hadn't had enough time; that there might never be enough time to get ready for driving that team myself.

Smoke had replaced the Krag's military rear sight with a Redfield peep. I put the bead on the end of the barrel between the buck's eye and his ear, then centered it in the window of the peep-sight. The rifle was almost as old as Harley. I wondered if the loose bolt and rust-pitted action would hold together one more time. *Remember: the breech block will push your fist, but not your fingers. The boy leans against the gun, slamming the block closed, his eyes on me— he knew, didn't he—sensing something was dead wrong, and Garrett stepping between us, yelling above the confusion to get that fuckin' lanyard in his hand . . .*

The front bead wavered back and forth across the deer's eye with each beat of my heart. I held my breath, saw him flick his ear, and started to squeeze the trigger, waiting for the flash to follow.

Harley lived on milk now and just about nothing else. He seemed annoyed at the fresh liver I fried for supper, and I had to admit it was rank. He lit the Aladdin and watched me eat. When I'd finished, he said, "Told you. That old rifle really busts 'em, don't it?"

"Yes," I answered, glancing at his temples, which in the past few days had caved in, leaving palm-sized hollows, "it really busts 'em."

"I'll tell you something else, and you remember it. Take care of your own, and don't never back off when you do." He narrowed his glittering eyes against the lamplight between us. "You know that day I was telling you about, when we left Bill Hirsch at his place? You know what he did after we'd gone?"

"No," I answered and pushed back from the table. I took out my pocketknife and began scraping at the dried blood caked around my fingernails. It seemed to me maybe I'd heard this before, but I couldn't remember what happened next in the story, and when I looked across the table at the spindle of drool that Harley was trying to spit clear of his chin into the grease can, I didn't much care.

I waited for him to draw his breath before I breathed. He looked up, and something I recognized crossed his face. He motioned me for water and I got him a dipperful from the tap. He drank and spit and worked at breathing. And I watched, breathing with him across the table, wishing my father would come, until he finally got his wind.

"Anyway," he said and set the empty dipper on the table. "That night it went down to maybe twenty-five below. Old Bill, God knows why, set out on foot for Slicker's. He only got a couple miles before he laid down in a drift and went to sleep."

Harley began tapping his fingers again on the table. Slow, one after the other, again and again. "Jumbo Hartz found him the next day and dug him out, figuring, you know, that Bill was froze to death."

I scraped the crusted blood from my thumbnail with my pocketknife. I'd hit the little buck in the side of his jaw the first shot, and I ran him most of a mile before I got the second one off. As I dug at the blood, I saw the jaw, dangling on shards of torn muscle, and the stub, too, of his exposed, shot-away tongue.

"But Bill wasn't dead at all," Harley said. "He was hung over pretty bad, and his feet, sticking out in the open all night, had frozen. Jumbo wanted to take him on to town, to see a doctor, but old Bill made Jumbo take him home instead." He spread his hands on the table, watching them now as if they were part of something remembered and remote. "And Bill stayed home," he said. "When his toes started to stink from the ganger in 'em, he took a tricorner file, and one by one, he sawed 'em off."

"Jesus, God!"

"That's right. You ask your dad. He'll tell you. He seen 'em plenty of times. The toes. Bill kept them around for years in a jar of alcohol."

I felt something poking me where my jeans pulled tight against my hip. I dug down in my pocket and pulled out the two spent Krag casings. The brass was tarnished a dull, crusty green. I remembered the night in the Clancy Bar, when I'd promised my brother I'd stay until he got back, remembered full force having decided to leave. I'd been younger then and strong, but the desire for life beyond these hills had been so much stronger; each day here had seemed such an agony of life postponed that I wondered why Summer had even bothered to ask. Unless he somehow knew he wouldn't be coming back.

"I'd better pull the hide off that buck before he freezes up," I said. I wanted to get back out into the cold, to breathe that cold deep and relieve myself of the stale, old-man smell of the house.

"Hold on right there," Harley said. "Bill Hirsch felt the same about doctors and town as I do. Now the lawyering is *done,* and I want you—" He broke off, bending again to cough, gathering the phlegm in his mouth like rage. "To promise me—"

"That's up to you and Smoke," I told him. "Nobody's going to take you to town until you're ready."

"You'll know when I'm ready, mister," he said.

I pulled the plank door closed behind me and felt the iron latch drop into place. I fumbled with the cord button loops on my mackinaw and tried to find, through the heavy falling snow, the outline of the homestead cabin, only a few yards away, that my grandfather had built on log runners to pull like a sled with his heavy teams from one quarter-section of sage and scrub to the next. I put my hands in my coat pockets and listened. I listened a long time, for the familiar growl of my father's four-by pulling hard against drifts; for the clank of his tire chains, which, since I could first remember, reminded me of distant horses pulling hard in harness. And gratefully, I listened last in the stillness to a welcome absence of wind.

34

"Ted's plowing Cutler Hill right now," Smoke said as he handed me the last sack of groceries. "He said he'd make a pass down here so you can get out." He swept snow from his boots on the plank porch and jerked his head toward the parlor. I shook my head and raised my hands. Without hesitation, he walked around me into the house and held the door for me.

He knelt beside Harley. "How are you doing, Dad?" he asked.

My grandfather held his hands together on his blanket-covered lap and nodded. Concentrated and remote, he lay his head back and closed his eyes. I watched them together as I slipped on my coveralls and gloves. I'd heard it said that Smoke had a lot of heart, and seeing him beside his father, I saw that it was so. Behind the wolfish face and hardened body lived a man capable of great and quiet tenderness.

"I'll be ready to load in a few minutes, Smoke," I said.

He looked around at me and nodded. "Go ahead. I'll bring the truck down in a little while."

"See you tomorrow then, Harley." I touched his arm.

Harley lifted his right hand and clasped mine with terrible strength. "Good luck on your calves," he said.

Rather than wean them, I'd decided to just take the spring calves to Butte. I'd fed for several days in the corral, catching a few of them each time until I had them all. At night, the cows bedded just beyond the rails, chewing their cuds and watching their offspring doomed by the fence.

I broke a few bales on the far side of the barn as Smoke backed his truck tight against the chute. The cows shuffled off to the hay without a backward glance.

"You won't get much for these culls," Smoke said, looking into the loading pen.

I had to admit they looked pretty scruffy in their winter hair, but they were grass-toughened and strong. All they needed was a chance. "He's not going to last long," I said.

"We'll be all right," Smoke answered. "I should have come to stay last week. I'll stay on now. Take a break. Stay down at my place if you want."

The calves milled and tried to hide in corners as we climbed the fence.

"Do you know where the old lady lives over there?"

"It's a couple blocks above the Greyhound station, before you start up the hill to Walkerville," Smoke answered. "Only building on the block, as I recall."

I helped myself to a Styrofoam cup of coffee from the urn beside the door. The auctioneer's magnified voice echoed in the naked ceiling beams above the sale ring as he ratcheted down the price until he found a bidder. A dozen shelly cows milled on the scale floor. Worn-out Holstein milkers, they sold quick and cheap. A door opened, the cows disappeared down an alleyway; the door closed, more hopeless cattle took their place.

The buyers marked their bid cards, their expressions bland as bankers. The sale was poorly attended; they were having a good day.

The three-story brick apartment house stood alone on a block of burned-out buildings whose shells resembled Smoke's aerial photographs of Berlin after the war. But here the residents had helped to vanquish themselves: the old North Side, honeycombed beneath its foundations with mine shafts and torched above ground by periodic insurance arson, was the end of the line for those who lived there last.

Inside, the walls were scarred from years of moving furniture and decades of family fights. Broken plaster exposed broken lath; gang names and slogans, written in spray paint, decorated the broken walls. I looked up the stairs and listened. Somewhere above me, someone coughed; a door slammed; a radio played a country song.

On the second-floor landing, a man in a bathrobe opened his door and leered at me. He flung open the robe, jabbered, and slammed his door. I climbed on.

It wasn't because I'd ever missed her; I'd hardly had time to meet her before she took off. Yet I recognized her when she opened the door, her body square in the loose kimono, her heavy face pale under powder. She held the door open and looked me up and down. "What'll it be today, sonny?" she said.

"I'm Jackson Heckethorn."

"Well, kiss my—" my mother said. She touched her hair with one hand. "And here—" She looked at me and laughed.

"I was in town. Thought I'd stop by for a minute."

"You surely did grow some since the last time I saw you." She closed her kimono around her breasts. "You want to come in?"

"Who's that?" a man asked behind her.

"Listen. You run down to the next corner and get some Winstons for me first. Give me five minutes."

When I returned from the bohunk grocery down the street, I found a black man sitting on the front steps lacing a pair of broken shoes. He looked up at me with milky eyes as I made to step around him.

"You her young-un, fo' sure?" he asked softly.

"Yeah, I guess I am."

"You guess?" he chuckled, hanging his lean arms over his sharp knees, letting his long black hands dangle loose. He seemed tickled by my answer, as if it satisfied an old and private joke. "You listen boy, that woman like an ol' cat, you see? All claws and hot pussy. I got trouble enough wifout young bucks hang'n' round."

"I won't be hang'n' round. This is a one-shot deal."

"She not quite straight sometimes, you understand?"

"If there's anything I understand, it's that. Must be in the blood."

"Tha's right, Doctor," he said and started off slack-limbed down the stairs. "Tha's right where it is. In the blood."

She tore the Winstons open with her thick fingers, leaned back against the cluttered sink, lit one, and offered me the pack. I shook my head. "How's What's-his-name?" she asked, pouring herself a water glass of red wine.

"He's pretty good. Got a broken leg and a girlfriend who's screwing half the town; either doesn't know or won't let on. Got his elk this year, cast and cane and all."

Her rooms were dark-walled and overfull. Bead curtains hung in doorways. Huge potted plants, like you used to see in flophouse lobbies, hunkered in dim corners. My mother wore men's slippers. Without looking, she flipped her ashes backhand toward the sink. "I heard he slowed down some. Even heard he quit boozing. You want a drink?"

"Whiskey?"

"Like father, like son. Sorry, just this wine."

"Thanks. I'll pass."

"You'd never have thought he would—slow down—the way he was when we got married. Always on the run. Always a can of Great Falls Select in one hand. Every weekend we'd go off to some godforsaken place and end up broke and drunk, sleeping in a horse trailer or under a truck, so he could rope calves with his rodeo buddies. Seemed he always had just enough money for entry fees and beer. Never enough for a motel or a hot shower. You should have seen us. We were regular gypsies."

"Sounds like the good life," I told her.

She shuddered, tipped her head back, and gazed at the dirty skylight overhead. "It got old fast." She stubbed out the cigarette, hugged herself, shook her curled hair. "I heard you were hurt in the war too," she said, looking at my face.

"I got hurt, but I never made it to the war."

"That's what ruined What's-his-name. Always hollering crazy in his sleep, dreaming searchlights and flak and chutes that wouldn't open."

"I remember that," I said. "I remember him dreaming."

"You were too small to remember anything," she said and fired another cigarette. She blew the smoke out her nose toward me, wondering, I thought, how much I did recall.

"So. Why'd you come here?" She squinted at me in the gloom. "I don't have anything."

"Don't know. Guess I wanted to see you was all."

"Well, here I am." She turned around slow. I could see the lumps of flesh above her hips, the red and purple veins in her legs. She raised her glass. "To me," she said.

"Do you need money or anything?"

She looked me over. "Oh, if you weren't mine, I'd take your money, believe in that."

I opened the door. "Why'd you leave?" I asked my mother.

She put a heavy arm on my shoulder, held the door with her other hand. I could smell the sweet wine on her breath and the smoke of many cigarettes. Her hennaed hair was gray at the roots. "Well," she said, and swayed against me, "I just couldn't stay."

I stopped at the Helsinki and had a few drinks. When the after-work crowd swelled the bar, I bought a fifth of Jack Daniel's and walked to the Finlen Hotel.

In the room, I pulled a chair to the window, watched the news on the TV with the sound off, and sat sipping whiskey as the gut-shot moon dived toward the Highland Mountains. It was an ass-backwards wake, yet for the first time I mourned my brother, who somehow seemed yet to live, and my family, the dead and the dying.

The maids woke me. I'd dozed with my boots on the heat register under the window, and by checkout time I'd stiffened like a corpse. They stood in the doorway, speaking quietly in Spanish as I hobbled out with my coat and hat. "Just here for the rodeo," I said, and they stared at me with mild, black-eyed contempt. I held the railing on the stairs, waiting for blood to find my feet before I started down. Inside the room, the girls stripped the untouched bed.

As I followed I-15 north out of town, I could see the hooded gallus frames and abandoned mine dumps above the old part of town. Below the highway lay the great gaping wound of the Berkeley Pit. A small mountain, once called The Richest Hill on Earth, had been leveled and hauled away. The digging had continued, and over the years the open pit grew wider and deeper, following the roots of the mountain until the giant machines on the bottom looked too small to be capable of further damage.

A town called Meaderville had once stood there, and in the town, a restaurant called the Rocky Mountain. A senator named Mansfield used to dine at the Rocky Mountain when he was home. I remembered eating there once myself, when Harley and Smoke had brought cattle to the livestock auction one fall when prices were high. That night they wore pearl Stetsons and wide grins. We had ravioli at the Rocky Mountain and watched for the senator, who never came.

By the time I was seven I'd known there were whores, and I also knew, that like the men who bought our cattle and took our checks, they were wealthy, well dressed, and lived in town. Mansfield had become an ambassador, and Meaderville was gone.

35

By the time we got back from the funeral home, the mound of chipped soil beside the grave had begun to freeze again. The backhoe man I'd hired simply left his bill weighted by a stone at the head of the grave before beginning the cold ride back to his truck and trailer on the county road. He'd done a good job. The grave was eight feet deep, just like I'd told him.

Lonnie, Ted, and I carried the coffin from Harley's pickup and rested it on planks above the hole. As the last of his friends made their way toward us from the four-wheel drives circling the little graveyard, I fastened the wire legs of a wreath in a nearby drift. The white flowers had frozen, and from a few feet away they were hard to see against the gray-white snow.

Chic Chalmers, the horseshoer, wheeled her father to where Smoke and I stood. Old man Chalmers twisted his head around, glowering up at us. His white hair lay coarse and uncombed over his blood-red ears. "Ain't *this* about right?" he demanded of no one in particular. "Hauled out here to his final glory in the back of a truck like a side of meat!" Chic shoved her hands into her coat pockets and winked at Smoke.

Amy and Annie Stevens stood across from us, looking cold in their black town clothes. Lonnie Ford put his arm around his mother, Ted Schillings joined his handsome wife, Laurie, and a few old folks I didn't know closed our ranks. A magpie flew from the bluff beyond the creek, gliding upstream like a shadow upon the snow.

Smoke cleared his voice and glanced around at Harley's friends. "He was . . . " Smoke said and stopped. Then, with the same determination he would use to face a bad job, he continued. " . . . clear-minded when he died. You all knew him most of your lives, so there isn't much point telling you what a good man he was."

Amy put her gloved hands to her face; her shoulders twitched beneath her thin coat like muscle under hide.

"He was hard on horses; he never forgot a grudge; he either liked you or he didn't. He lived up here by himself and did pretty much what he wanted. When he got sick, he said he intended to die here. He wanted to die with dignity, and he did."

Smoke noticed the backhoe bill fluttering under the stone and hesitated. "He liked good cattle and he loved this damn place. First and last he was true to himself." Smoke looked around the circle of faces. "Does anybody have anything else to say?"

"How about amen?" Chalmers offered, rearing back in his wheelchair.

Smoke picked up two lengths of hawser line. "Then would a couple of you give me a hand?" he asked.

We looped the old hay rope under the coffin, kicked the planks away from the hole, and jostled Harley into the ground. The burnished tin box seemed too light to contain a man.

"We've got hot coffee and coffee cake at the house," Smoke said, coiling the two-inch lines around his left arm. "Let's all go warm up."

Everyone stood a moment longer, relieved that the graveside business was over. But when I pulled a number-two shovel from Harley's pickup, Amy slumped into the snow on her knees. She put her fists against her ears and began keening, a high, quavering wail that stood my neck hair on end.

"Give 'em hell, Hotpants," Chalmers said. He opened his horsey old mouth and laughed smoke rings into the freezing twilight air.

Amy's knifing voice cut the embarrassed silence around me as she inched forward on her knees, her eyes pinched, her hands running like spiders through her hair. Ted Schillings took his wife's arm and together they turned away. Chalmers' gray face burned a hot, mottled red. "Damn sight more than I expected outa her," he said to me.

Annie knelt beside her mother, and I was surprised when Smoke bent and gently helped the old lady to her feet. "Goddamn you anyway, Harlan," Amy said straight out, as if her grief had turned back into a long cherished anger, and she'd finally found the courage or anguish or outrage to address its source.

As Smoke led her toward Annie's Jeep, Chalmers gazed at me with wide, surprised eyes, as if he'd forgotten where he was. People moved off toward their vehicles. No one except Amy wept. Harley hadn't been that kind of man.

Lonnie touched my arm. "He taught me to ride," he said. "And swear."

As the sad line of secondhand pickups drove to the house, I took a post bar and broke chunks of dirt from the mound. I shoveled slowly, listening to the frozen clods strike the hollow metal box. When his mother had died in 1917, Harley and his father had wrapped her in canvas and waited for a thaw. And when Harley's father killed himself that spring, Harley was breaking horses at Camp Dodge, Iowa.

Snow lay corniced over most of the creek, except where I'd chopped water holes through the ice for my cows. An owl mumbled in the dark timber, and the first stars glazed the western sky above Sheep Mountain. I shoveled until the grave was half full, stepped in, and walked in small, trudging circles, tamping the soil tight. Coyotes called to the airliner gliding past on its final descent to Helena, their giddy yodels trailing off as soon as the plane had passed.

I walked to Summer's grave and lifted a burlap bag I'd hidden behind his stone. From it I took the mason jug I'd discovered in the cellar and placed it in the grave at the foot. At the head, I arranged the horned white skull of a Hereford bull.

It was dark by the time I rounded off the last of the dirt. When I picked up the wreath, the flowers broke like glass. The owl called again, and voices drifted to me from the buildings as people prepared to leave. The lights in Harley's house burned in the night. Clearly, I heard Chalmers say " . . . anything with hair."

I noticed Carlisle's book beside the cloth-covered TV and picked it up. He looked tough in the picture on the back cover. Behind him a sign said NO SHIRT, NO SHOES, NO SERVICE. I took the book into the kitchen, lit the lamp I'd learned to read by, and began. Around midnight I closed it and stared at the cover. The story was about a man who loved a place and a woman, and while he lost both, almost managed to keep himself intact. Set in the West and disguised as a hard-boiled detective novel, it was really a book about caring for things you couldn't have.

The door to my room had been closed all day, and the bunk was cold as snow as I shivered down between the sheets. I pulled the horsehide robe up and, smelling the stale tanning agents in the leather, wondered if it was really the roan in Harley's picture like he'd said, or if that was only another of his twists.

The blankets warmed, and as I dozed, I listened to the roof beams crack above my head, to the iron rooster creak as it weathervaned in the wind. The old house grew around me into a clapboard mansion of spiraling staircases and long oblique hallways. Smoke joined me on a broad landing where several dim halls met above an enclosed, chandeliered mezzanine. Yet in the dream I knew it was Harley's house.

Smoke and I wander apart. I explore the halls, feeling a prickly elation sharpened by fear. In one room a bull elk hangs head-down from the ceiling, blood pooled under his nose; in another, workhorses supported by broad leather bellybands stand with their shaggy heads low, their eyes half closed. The hay bunks along the log walls are empty, the manger poles rough where the horses have chewed the wood. I turn to find Smoke and see him standing beside an airport security guard, looking rawboned and worn. Closer, I notice how his long hair has grayed. He brushes the sleeves of a shirt I recognize; when we shake, he is careful of his arthritic hand. Outside, we cross the parking lot toward a battery of 105s. "We're just going to shoot the living hell out of them," Smoke says. The girl I'd known in Canada rises on her toes to kiss a man carrying a briefcase. When I speak to her, she disappears in a muzzle flash; the howitzer rears in a hail of sparks, lies down in slow motion on its back, aiming upside down in the wrong direction, its tires boiling smoke. And a roan horse lopes past me toward the blind corral, his tail and mane bright with flames.

36

The telephone rang as I dozed with my legs over the side of the galvanized tub. I pulled a towel over my shoulders and stood, twisted another around my hips, and stepped onto the cold floor. Soap ran from my hair and stung my eyes as I walked toward the telephone. There was a pause when I answered, then the familiar, muted voice: "Jackson?"

"I was just thinking about you," I said, shivering in a draft blowing through an unchinked space between two logs in the west wall. "How's Victoria and the big-city life?"

I rubbed my cold hair with one hand, leaning over the Windsor stove for warmth. Beads of water hissed and sizzled as they struck the cast-iron lid.

"Jack," she said.

I toweled off my upper body, noticing with satisfaction the new roundness of my shoulders, the extra inch of hard muscle slabbed on my chest and arms, the ripples beneath the skin on my stomach. I felt very fit, shivering in the heat of the glowing stove. "Go ahead, pal. I'm here."

"I hate this," she said.

I wiped the soap from my face and eyes and shook my head, again spraying the stove with droplets.

"I . . . haven't been . . . completely—Oh, shit! How are you? Are you all right?"

"I'm fine. What's wrong?"

Her voice came in a harsh rush, like water freed behind

broken ice, like wind through an open door. "I must tell you that . . . I'm not . . . here alone. I've been staying with a friend who teaches here. Oh, damn! I didn't plan on this. I didn't do it on purpose, but I've been so . . . I needed something, someone—"

I opened my stinging eyes. The familiar parlor, bathed in the soft light of the lamp, seemed to turn slowly around me. Outside, I could hear the wind rolling off the timbered ridges, tearing across the fields and flats, nudging the old house.

"I was going to get a place of my own, but . . . he's asked me to stay. And I've told him yes."

I opened my mouth to answer or to breathe. The windows rattled and I could hear snow whipping against the glass. Gently, I put the receiver back on the cradle.

I dressed, went upstairs to the hall closet, and from behind some boxes of paperbacks, pulled the heavy, zippered bag I'd used for a riggin sack. In my room, I spread the contents on my bunk: the association bronc saddle and flank strap and rein, the rosin sock, Ace bandages, awl and lacings, and the fancy chaps with Summerfield's initials stamped on the orange and black skirts. I straddled the saddle on the floor, put my boots in the forward-thrust steel stirrups, and bent my knees as much as I could. I closed my eyes and, holding the braided rein high with my right hand, nodded my head. I turned my toes out and tried to imagine the horse turning away from the chute gate, leaving the ground, and lunging into the air. I held my legs out, the points of the spurs along his shoulders until he landed, then began in my mind to cantle-spur him for points. But instead of the roar of the crowd, I heard only the red iron roof above me banging in the wind, and the telephone ringing on and on downstairs.

.　　.　　.

I began cutting ten feet downstream from Ted Schillings'
fence, where Jackson Creek gurgled under two feet of
gorged and air-pocketed ice. I sawed into a jungle of en-
twined aspen and willow, cottonwood and alder, cutting my
way through green wood and dead alike, cutting my way
toward the sound of water. The meadow, first cleared by
Harley's father, had once grown hay to a tall man's chest.
Now even the creek itself was hidden in places, buried under rotting logs, tangles of wild rose, and miles of inter-
meshed creepers.

I sawed and split sound wood and ricked it in conical
stacks to haul away later. Limbs, brush, and punky wood I
piled on old car tires. After the first couple of shifts, I managed to keep at least one big fire going day and night. I had
about fifteen acres to clear; there wasn't any rush, the future
was no further than my next fire. My closest contact with
people was with passengers on the jetliner I waved to every
afternoon and the Fish and Game Cessna that sometimes
tipped its wings as it passed. I kept the brushfires burning,
the red gate locked, and the Krag loaded.

I could hear the creek whispering below the ice. One hot
August in five, Jackson Creek dried up, leaving only mud
holes and landlocked tadpoles. There would be no new
creeks, I knew, only—as the prairie and hills were carved
by roads and squared into house lots—more users.

Smoke called between his trips east, yet I lost track of the
days. January passed into February. I began sleeping afternoons. At dusk, I stirred my fires awake, heaped on aspen
and willow, and watched the sparks fly up in the night. I fed
my cows in the mornings, before turning in. A few, beginning to make bag, hung off by themselves. Seeing them
readying to calve again surprised me, as if I'd supposed
them as barren as myself.

·   ·   ·

"Hey, Easy Money," a voice called from the darkness beyond the fire. I swung around, holding my ax with both hands.

Ted Schillings stepped into the light and I put the ax against an old yellow pine I intended to let stand.

"Come on and warm up," I said and backed to the fire.

Ted handed me a foil-wrapped loaf of his wife's homemade bread and spread his hands before the heat.

"I hear you're thinking of selling out," I said.

He turned his back to the blaze and leaned his head to one side. "I don't know what to think, with things the way they are. What are you going to do?"

"Winter here, I guess. Could hit the road with the first Chinook. Start at those early indoor shows down south, work my way north until I learn to ride again."

"Hard row to hoe."

I shook my head. "It's like anything else that gets in your blood. Gambling, booze, cattle."

"I'm glad that one never got in mine. How's your dad doing?"

"Hauling hay. Got his cast off. Don't see much of him. Are you going to sell, do you think?"

"I may turn loose of some ground. Tanners have submitted a plan to the County Commission to develop all their ground, not just along Casey Creek."

"But not your home place though?"

"I'm just not sure, Jack. That's partly up to my accountant and the bank and some lawyers." Ted seemed restless and I let it drop, knowing he had to think of his family.

"Been meaning to come down. We see your fires up home at night, but you know how it is when you're feeding."

"Sure. I kind of miss it . . . feeding out a good bunch and claving."

"It never quits," Ted answered. "Every year a fella figures he'll do better, have better luck, get a better price come fall. But it's always the same, or nearly always. You work hard at it when you're young, build up your place, breed up your stock, work on your fields. Then the price of beef goes down. One day you look outside and it's winter again, the whole thing to go through over, and you just don't care. You come to the point where you can see you aren't gaining an inch, that the fence posts you put in a few years back have rotted off, the barn's leaning, the kids growing up or gone."

I wished for a cigarette, although I seldom thought of them now. And I nodded at what Ted had to say, because I'd already seen that it was true.

I piled tree after tree onto the fire, heating it to the core. As I paused between armloads, I watched figures struggling in the heat-warped and iridescent embers: distant horsemen rode wavering from log to log, and faces appeared that turned the fire cold. Harley's father had plowed flint scrapers, sling rocks, and buffalo skulls—filled with rich loam like great horned cups—from the root-bound soil. Since my earliest childhood wanderings around the place I had sensed them there. I wondered if Harley had felt them too, when he came back to the abandoned place and the worst winter in living memory; I tried to conjure what it had been for him, the poverty and unexpected young man's loneliness he must have faced, and I wondered how he'd found the courage to go on when his father had not. *Cattle had been in the house, stepped through the floor in places, busted up the furniture. Thieves had cleaned the place out: my dad's shotguns, our lamps and chairs, most of the tools, even the lids off the stove. I chiseled their names on the only thing I had for headmarkers, a broken leaf from the kitchen table.*

37

Four dollars and ninety-five cents, the original price, written in carpenter's pencil and covered with layers of varnish, was clearly visible on the toe board of the snowshoe as I knelt to unfasten it. I shook snow from the webbing and stood the pair in a drift beside the back door. It had taken me two hours to lumber over the drifts to Amy's; by the time I arrived, the evening star was bright in the west. I pulled off my mittens and knocked.

Annie looked through the kitchen window, then opened the door. "Sergeant Preston!" she said. "What are you doing out on foot? It's fifteen below!"

"Trailing Lucky Pierre Lavecque, ma'am, but I need to rest my faithful huskies before pursuing him farther into the frozen North."

"On, King, on!" Annie echoed and hummed a couple bars of the theme song.

"Truth is, I got tired of talking to the stove. Where's Amy?"

"Momma caught a cold that night at Harley's funeral. She doctored here at home, but it got worse and worse until it turned into pneumonia. She's been in the hospital three days now."

I pulled the felt liners from my packs and stood the lug-soled shells beside the stove. Annie shook back her heavy

hair and watched me with her head tipped to one side as I
pulled the liners back on. My nose and ears began to tingle.
"How bad is she?" I asked.

"Bad enough. Intensive care."

"Are you getting by okay?"

"It's tough, trying to feed and get to the hospital every
day. Long as I don't have any breakdowns, I'll be all right."

"I've got plenty of time, if you need help."

Annie punched me on the arm. "You're on, Constable.
Help me feed tonight. How about some groceries first?"

I set the table in the dim front room as Annie banged
around in the kitchen. The sizzling smells of bacon and venison, onions, and potatoes reminded me that I hadn't been
eating. "Anything new on your lawsuit?" I asked, leaning in
the kitchen door and watching Annie bustle about the stove.

"It's going to court, we're just waiting for a date. They're
wrong and know it. They can't even look me in the eye.
They're bulldozing us, and all *our* lawyer can talk about is
settling out of court."

I frowned at her as she stood with her hands on her hips.
She pushed her hair back and with a sharp motion of her
head flung it over her shoulder. "Which is the same as paying for something that's already ours. I don't know whose
side he's on any more." She lifted a frying pan in each hand
and brushed by me. "Come and get it," she said.

At the table, Annie passed a bowl of brown gravy and our
fingers touched for a moment. I took the gravy boat and
looked at her.

"What?" Annie asked, smiling wide-eyed and pretty.

"I haven't seen anyone—a woman—in so long, I feel like
I might go crazy."

"You sweet-talking man," she said, laying her warm hand
on my arm.

We ate without speaking again, keeping our eyes on our
plates. When we'd finished, I cleared the table while Annie
went into a bedroom to put on her outside clothes. I scraped

the plates, filled the sink with soapy water, and began to wash the cups and pans. The kitchen looked the same as when Summer and I had helped them hay the place when we were in high school. The porcelain tomatoes over the stove, the tiny pantry with mousetraps set on the floor, the .22 pump leaning in one corner. It hadn't changed, and I felt the reckless kid in me again, the six-foot, one-hundred-and-forty-pound geek who had been one hay-mowing dude.

Outside, Annie backed her Jeep to an old-fashioned bobsled. I dropped the kingpin through the clevis on the hardwood tongue, and she pulled into the stack yard, where we wrestled frosty bales to the sled, chopping frozen ones apart with a post bar. Amy's Angus lined out at a slow trot from the field below the house. Their breath rose above their frosted backs, their hooves squealing on the frozen snow as they came.

I rode the sleigh into the field until Annie slowed, then began the ritual of cutting strings and pitching fragrant slices of hay to the eager cattle. The little Jeep churned along, its tire chains clinking like bells as the rising moon blued the snowbound flat. I remembered again feeding with Harley and my brother; the restlessness to hit the road that I'd felt then seemed diminished, and that nagged at me. It worried me to be content with what had once seemed so empty.

We hauled two loads, then unhooked the sleigh. Annie drove her Jeep into a pole-sided shed and plugged in the electric engine heater. She slapped her mittens together as we walked toward the house and smiled up at me. "Two's sure better than one on nights like this," she said, putting her arm around my waist.

We leaned against each other and listened to the movements of the distant cattle as they milled at their feed. I noticed one of the stars moving and pointed to it. "Good-bye, Mr. Spock," I said.

Annie watched the satellite cross the heavens. "I wonder what it's like," she said finally, "to be so far away."

"Should have asked me a few months ago."

"I used to think stars were people who had died, you know, when I was little. A star for each person who'd ever lived. I even picked ones for people I loved. Summer's is over there, in Orion's belt."

"I didn't know," I said.

Annie squeezed my arm. "There's a lot you don't know, Scooter."

She undressed me slowly in the light of a single candle. I thought of the satellite curving through space and what Annie had said about dying. I closed my eyes and drifted, feeling the aching weight of life slipping away.

I woke before first light and felt her breasts against my side, her warm hair upon my arm. I kissed her eye; she snuffled, slid her hand across my chest, and smiled in her sleep.

"Annie," I whispered.

"Hi," she mumbled, snuggling against me.

"Wake up, I want to ask you something."

She began to snore softly, her lips slightly parted.

"Hey!" I rolled onto her and grabbed her wrists. "If you don't give me the deed to your ranch, I'll blow you all to bits!"

Annie looked at me through half-open eyes. "Hummm?"

"Saw you in half down at the sawmill, or maybe run a train over you!"

Annie opened her eyes wide. "Not the sawmill!" She flung her head from side to side on the pillow. "Oh, help, help!" she cried. "Help, help?"

"No, wait! Maybe I've got the wrong part. I could *save* the ranch! That's it. We'll get together and I'll save the ranch."

Annie's eyes cleared.

"Call me Dudley. Let's team up and make this here country safe for your young-uns."

Annie rolled from under me, and kneeling, kissed my cheek. She looked at me awhile, and kissed me again. "You don't know who I am, do you, Scooter?"

"I guess I do, I've known you all my life. It's not Summerfield?"

"Hush," she said and pushed me onto my back. She lay down, slid one leg across my waist and put a hand on my cheek. "I'm your goddamn aunt or something."

"Say again?"

"Lay still. Harley and Mom weren't always old and worn out. They were like us, maybe. I remember them together when I was real small."

"No," I said, and saw it was absolutely true, saw Harley and Amy again at the kitchen window through my rainbow of sparks as I pumped the emery wheel against iron.

"Harley used to come here late at night and sometimes stay." Annie pulled a quilt over us and turned to face the wall.

"But why did they keep it secret? You saw Amy the night we buried Harley."

"Momma says it was because of your grandma."

"But she was dead."

"Not to Harley she wasn't."

I lay back, closing my eyes. "Who else knows?"

"Just about everybody in the county," Annie said. "Everybody now, I guess."

I looked around the room and watched the gray light of day border the curtains on the window at the foot of the bed. "Was that why Summer left so sudden?"

"Yes," Annie said. "It was."

38

I splashed diesel fuel on one side of a barn-sized brush pile, then walked back, lighting the oily fuel with a flaming pitch root. The fire spread, leaping from limb to limb, licking at car tires scattered inside until the draft created by the increasing heat roared up, carrying sparks high into the night. During the past few weeks I'd managed to clear several acres, but it didn't look like I'd ever get it all.

Working by the light of the flames behind me, I began to lay the next night's fire. And I began to wonder why I was fooling with this still, why I kept at this clearing of brush, which would never pay me a dime. Yet that had been Harley's dilemma too, I supposed. What to do, in order to survive, when he returned and found himself alone. And what had he done? As far as I knew, he'd taken up where he'd left off, cutting cordwood and selling to Boone's wood yard, located where the new library was now being built. He had worked the teams Tom Flavven had boarded for him while he was at Camp Dodge, and he'd built the big corral. Running on guts and desperation, Harley had gone after the inbred, cross-blooded horses that were wild and rank and dangerous in ways you don't see much anymore.

I sat down to rest on a rotting cottonwood log, watched the fire consume living and dead wood alike, and thought about my neighbors, who faced, whether they would admit it or not, the same certainty of dispossession as the Indians Harley had seen camped that winter where the Colonial Inn now stood. Amy Stevens, still in the hospital, one day better, one day worse; Ted Schillings, work-worn and facing an uncertain future; Lonnie Ford, hanging on to what he knew; Smoke, alone again, whether he realized it or not. And what had trapped them was so simple, so clear. Change. Change accelerating beyond their wildest dreams, until each trip they took to town showed them new evidence of their hopeless way of life. New basements, new power lines and survey crews on land that hadn't changed in recent geological time.

I wondered if what was happening here was also spreading across the rest of Montana, across the entire West. And if it was, where would I go? What place could I find that would take me in as this one had?

I heard the drone of an engine and the tapping of side chains against fenders. Car lights touched the tops of trees beyond the creek, and then I saw the truck itself. Smoke drove into the circle of firelight, climbed from his truck, and walked toward me, swaying as he came. He held up a quart bottle of Wild Turkey, and his teeth flashed in the firelight.

He tossed me the bottle, turned, and pissed into the hot ashes at the outer edge of the fire. "Looked like the whole place was on fire from Harris Hill," he said.

"What were you doing out there?"

"Drinking good liquor and looking at the damn country."

I uncorked the bottle, raised it to my lips, and took a pull. The heat of it in my throat satisfied a craving I hadn't let myself admit was there. "Kind of fell off the wagon, huh, old man?"

He turned his eyes toward me without moving his head. The sloped shoulders, the wild, jet-black hair, the eyes, hidden partly under heavy brows—in the flickering light, he looked like some kind of primitive man, waiting for the fire to singe a joint of meat. I laughed at him, all liquored up and sober at the same time.

"Fuck you, boy," he said, "and your red horse." He held

out his hand for the whiskey. I raised it instead to my lips and watched erratic bubbles rise in the bottle as I drank.

"Hey!" Smoke said. "That's sipping whiskey."

I caught my breath, bubbled the bottle again, and although I could feel the fire trying to come back up, hit it one last long time. When I couldn't stand any more, I handed him back the bottle and wiped my eyes.

"There ain't any way you're going to catch up," Smoke said, watching me as he tipped the bottle.

I held onto myself to keep the whiskey down. "We'll just find out, won't we, Smoke?" I watched as he swayed before the fire. It had been twenty years since I'd seen him take a drink. "Moonshine," I said. "Here's to you and the rest of the world's great lovers."

He pulled his Copenhagen can, dropped it, and kicked it into the fire. "I should have seen it, and maybe I did," he said. He bubbled the Turkey himself and when he lowered the bottle, a bead of liquor ran down his chin. He took another pull and passed it. "I knew about her from the start. But I figured I could change her chippy'n' ways by just being good to her and showing her a good time." He turned his back on me, held his hands to the fire, and said, "Found out I was wrong. Ever happen to you?"

I tossed the cork into the fire and took a shallow sip. "No. Yes."

Smoke turned abruptly, looking at me with his glittering eyes. "It was all in my head. She's been . . . Hank Simpson finally straightened me out this afternoon, damn him." He swept his hand toward the clearing I'd made, stood quiet for a while, then asked, "What got you started on this?"

"Something to do. Harley mentioned it."

Smoke belched and walked to my log and sat beside me. "We cut horse hay in here when I was a kid. Kill a cottontail a round with the horse mower. Don't see rabbits like that now."

"Make pasture, wouldn't it?"

"Sure. But I could clear this whole mess in a couple days with a Cat."

"Not like I'm doing it you couldn't."

He looked me over, had a sip, held out the whiskey. "Maybe not, kid," he said quietly.

I raised the Turkey to my lips, washed my mouth, and spat into the snow. "I'm twenty-seven years old," I said.

Smoke pointed at me and laughed, and we laughed together, passing the bottle, for a time just watching the brush collapse into embers and letting the night wane in pure foolishness.

"What do you want?" Smoke asked with a jerk of his head, a crooked smile cutting his shadowed face.

"I've been telling you since I got off that airplane last September. Where the hell have you been?"

"Just take it easy now. I've got some papers in the truck that concern you. We have to make some decisions, got to see Harley's lawyer too. That would be Wednesday."

"What day is this?"

"Saturday. Except up here. Hasn't been a Saturday night on this place since I was your age. Middle o' the week year round. Look forward to that, see how you feel. This hellhole wore out some pretty good people. And for what? A narrow grave, just like the song says. And that's all. I'll tell you, I've about had it with this fucking ranch!" He underlined the word *ranch* with his fist like he thought it was a joke. "Now say we sell this rock pile, put that money in certificates and bonds, and live off the interest, you won't have to get up at three in the morning to pull a forty-dollar calf."

"You're right." I stood and began throwing the burnt ends of limbs and logs into the center of the fire. The flames swelled, clutching at the charred wood. "On the other hand, a man could make wages by just putting steers on grass up here," I said.

"You might break even, if the market didn't fall too far between when you bought and when you sold. And you pasture the place, you got no hay come winter."

"You've got the hay."

I could see the notion flicker on his face. He'd been around the cattle game long enough to have a nose for blood. His hesitation made the whole idea seem possible. "You've got grass all right. But do you know how much it would cost to fence that open ground?"

The whiskey burned in my face. "Harley bought the posts and wire," I said.

Smoke turned his eyes to me. Slowly, he said, "Harley what?"

"In the milk house. Steel posts, barbed wire, staples, and twist-ons. Everything we need except corner posts."

A fine snow began to fall, windless and dry. The creek chugged under the ice behind us, and I could see the first gray hint of false dawn.

"You got no water," Smoke finally said. "You got guts but no water." He stood and pitched the bottle into the heart of the fire, and the last of the liquor flashed in a blue-white arc back toward his hand.

Smoke stared at me with his whiskey-wild eyes, then turned abruptly, fell to one knee at the edge of the fire, and retched into the white ashes. Hidden coals sputtered and hissed. His shoulders heaved, the disturbed ashes flew into his face, and after a while I saw that he was weeping. I looked toward the bluff beyond the creek, just able to make out the trees on the graying skyline. Smoke lifted his streaked, ash-whitened face. "You think you've found something here, and maybe you're not wrong. But *this* is your inheritance," he said, and threw a handful of hot ashes against the morning sky.

J am that round in there! Move, damn your eyes. Ain't nothin' to be scared of out here 'cept me!" Garrett leans over the boy, veins bulging in his sunburned neck as he curses, threatens, praises, rants, and lies . . . Garrett making the boy's life a nightmare, making him take the lanyard, to just by-God prove it's safe. And the boy, who'd had trouble with the fuse, looking not at Garrett anymore, but at me, his eyes trying to find something safe in mine, something he can hang on that will keep him together as his fear tries to pull him apart.

I glance again at my watch, thinking of the miles across Montana, Wyoming, Colorado, New Mexico, wondering where in all that distance you might be—Texas, maybe even Oklahoma by now. And it's late afternoon, most of our ammo fired, only a few more rounds to put in the air before my trainees will begin to clean the guns. I need to shower and change, to pick up some Jack Daniel's black and steaks, maybe clean the bathroom at my place off post. Six hours . . . *What?* something working in the back of my mind, something behind the fatigue and dust and confusion around me.

Garrett pointing his finger, saying something lost in the noise. The rigid boy clenches the lanyard in his shaking hand, *What the hell?* like even on his first day he's seen something . . . As the order comes the boy hesitates, like I thought he would, and I clamp the fuse spanner in my hand.

Garrett raising one arm, the boy's eyes locked on mine, the lanyard going taut . . .

A flash like a second sun at the end of the muzzle and the invisible fist of concussion . . . weeds and dry grass, and I'm back up, on my knees, groping my face, my hands finding blood as the howitzer lies down on its back. My fingers in my mouth, finding the sliver of shiny steel. Pieces of my teeth in my open palm, some of the tooth chips seeming touched by decay.

My buddy Garrett, a silly startled grin on that wind-roughened West Texas face, walking toward me from the burning gun. "Fuse?" he asks and sits carefully down, his fatigues bubbling blood beneath his collar and down his arms. "Fuse?" he says again and I kneel with him, as if we're about to pray.

I hear the battery's rounds hiccup beyond the ridge, see men running from the corner of my eye. And in the smoking native grass around the trails of my piece, Billy Garrett and three of my trainees demonstrate the "hands-on method" of dying.

I opened my eyes, the echoes of my voice still ringing in the bare log room. Sunshine streamed through the dormer windows, a warm wind melting the icicles hanging beyond the glass. I touched my face, my hair. There was no blood, no pain, only sweat and the smell of willow smoke on my skin.

"Houseboat?" Smoke asked as he locked the doors on his pickup. "You mean Harley's ark? Sure, I know where it came from. Harley did some plowing for this joker down by Winston, before Canyon Ferry flooded the valley. Eight head of horses, gang blows, like that. He stayed down there a couple weeks, working as long as the horses could work. Come to find out when he got done, the guy didn't have any money, just that old boat." Smoke unbuttoned his topcoat and loosened his tie. "So Harley got some iron-wheeled axles under it, hooked on to 'er with his horses and pulled it home. Every spring he'd say, 'Now if we get'—and he'd name off a string of jobs long as your arm—'done, we'll pull that boat out to the Missouri and take us a little cruise.' But every year something would break down or somebody'd get hurt or sick or some damn thing, and we never did take a trip. Only thing ever really happened was Harley painted my mom's name on the bow. But he talked about going each spring till I went into the army. In fact, he talked about leaving a lot when I was a kid. As if you *could* get away when you're milking fifty cows twice a day."

We walked down Sixth Avenue toward the Power Block and our appointment with Harley's attorney, a Chinook wind working our hair. Smoke, I had to admit, looked pretty sharp in a suit.

"You decide what the hell you're doing yet?" he asked.

"I think so."

"Well, you better know so. You never know about family deals. Or wills. Lawyers will call day night, then act like you're dumb 'cause you can't see the stars."

A block south of us, a crane swung a wrecking ball against a brick wall. The wall didn't move. Smoke worried his tie and punched his shirttail into his pants as he limped along. "I'll tell you a little family history you may not know," he said. "After my granddad Kahler's wife left him, I used to go stay with him up on Warm Springs Creek, like you used to stay with Harley. He was a little rough, but he got lonesome, and he liked kids. We got along good. Well, when his health finally failed, he came to live with us. Used to sleep in that room where you store your wood. Died there, in fact."

The crane turned toward the street, the iron ball spinning like the bobber on a perch line. "My folks took care of him. Harley got doctors to come out, my ma kept him comfortable, made him feel at home. When he died, he willed his place to my mother, plus a couple thousand dollars in cash.

"Back comes Jake's wife, my mother's mother. She'd been gone ten years by then and was married to some bum from Butte. She hired a lawyer and contested the will. In court, under oath, she testified that my mother wasn't their child. She swore my mother was a half-breed orphan who had been left on their doorstep."

The crane turned, the boom swinging silently across the street. The ball, like a child on the end of a line of kids playing crack the whip, hurtled out of control into the brick wall. Wood squealed, a geyser of red dust spurted upward, the wall wobbled but stood.

"It hurt my mother," Smoke said. "And Mrs. Kahler won the suit. She ended up with the place *and* the money."

"What about birth certificates, hospital records, that kind of thing?"

"I don't know," Smoke answered. "I was too small to understand the particulars. The point is, the old lady's lawyers convinced a jury of our friends and neighbors that my mother was a bastard. And if they can do that, you'd better pay attention when we get to this guy's office."

I glanced at him as we waited for the light to change on Last Chance Gulch. With his jet hair tied back, his high cheekbones and hawk nose seemed to stretch his face skin tight. He was fair skinned, but he had the blackest hair of any white man I'd ever seen. He looked a little like old man Kahler in the pictures Harley had, but you couldn't tell. I was pretty dark myself.

40

A. C. Vickery's wood-paneled office on the fourth floor of the Power Block had the somber look of old money. My palm was sweaty as he shook my hand and motioned Smoke and me toward three leather chairs clustered to one side of his desk. He was a large man, perhaps sixty, comfortable in his surroundings. On a pedestal, next to the east-facing window, stood a Remington-like bronze of a bronc rider and horse in midair above a coiled rattlesnake.

"Call me A. C.," Vickery said, seating himself between us and opening a manila folder with Harley's name on the cover. "This is fairly clean, so it shouldn't take too long." He talked for a few minutes about the recent visits Harley had paid him, allowing himself to digress on his personal impressions of Harley. I noticed that he addressed himself mostly to me, including Smoke the way a banker would involve a consenting parent about to cosign a car loan for a teenage son.

The will itself was brief, although an inch of other documents had been appended behind it. As the lawyer read the initial pages, I found myself studying the bronze cast behind him, searching details in the surprised, outflung arm of the rider—his quirt flying straight back behind his open hand—and the exaggerated definition of the rising horse's chest and muscled legs.

"So it's really a matter of money and land," A. C. said. "Mr. Heckethorn senior"—he motioned to Smoke—"is to

receive the monies accumulated in various accounts here in
Helena, and you, sir," he said, looking at me, "are to receive
the properties of the Heckethorn ranch, located in Jefferson
County, including the land, buildings, brands, livestock,
and equipment on or belonging to said ranch."

I couldn't decide if the rider, thrown out of balance and
standing in his stirrups above the horse's bowed neck, would
last the next second or not. It looked plausible one moment,
utterly impossible the next.

"Do you understand?" A. C. asked me.

"Yes, I understand."

"Of course there are a few irregularities in the land ab-
stracts and titles, which Mr. Heckethorn, with my help, set
about correcting before his death. Are you familiar with the
problems to which I refer?"

I glanced at Smoke, who nodded and said, "The ground
in my mother's name?"

"That's correct. It will be several months before that is
completely cleared up, although at this time, I see no real
problems beyond the unusual amount of time between Mrs.
Heckethorn's death and the transfer of title to Mr.
Heckethorn. From your grandfather to you shouldn't be a
problem if . . . when we clear this up."

I stood and walked to the tall window overlooking Last
Chance Gulch. Even at this height, people on the sidewalks
looked smaller, more fragile than from below

A. C. closed the folder behind me. After a moment's hesitation, he said, "In the event that you may wish to sell part
or all of this property, I've been authorized by one of my
associates—who prefers to remain unnamed at the present—to communicate an offer. That is, if you would be
interested."

I watched cars turning up the steep hill on Sixth Avenue.
"How much?" I asked.

"Well, I'm afraid I don't have a figure at this time. That

could be worked out, I'm sure, if you indicated an interest in selling."

A white Cadillac convertible swung left at the light. The top was down, and I could make out the bullet-necked driver, one hand on the wheel, his elbow resting on the open-windowed door. Beside him, standing in the seat with his disfigured little face thrust into the wind like a hound, seeming even smaller than before, rode Bean, like a malignant little boy.

"That's not much of an offer," I said, watching Carlisle and his smoking Dumpster disappear up Sixth Avenue.

"I'm sure I'm safe in saying it would be six figures," A. C. said.

I looked back at the bronze statue—*He was hard on horses; he never forgot a grudge; he either liked you or he didn't*—and decided the rider could make it after all. "Just have Tanners call me, A. C., and I'll tell them no myself."

"As you wish," he said and stood. "My secretary has some things for you to sign, but I think that about wraps it up for now." His hand was firm and dry when we shook.

Smoke slapped me on the shoulder in the open mezzanine outside the office. "Right on the money, Jack," he said, and grinned. The balconylike landings of the exposed floors below reminded me vaguely of something; then I remembered registering for the draft on the floor beneath us when I'd turned eighteen. "Next thing is to get a different lawyer, before old A. C. ties it up in court," Smoke added.

I ran my hand along the hardwood banister above the hollow core of the building, remembering my dream of Harley's house.

"How about a drink, Smoke?" I asked. "This time we can start together."

In three days the unceasing Chinook wind bared each ridge and filled the gulches with white-foamed water. Ice-choked

culverts turned the water back until it rose to the level of the
road and ran on in urgent, parallel streams down deeply
rutted tire tracks. Annie rode beside me, one boot on the
dashboard for balance. I geared down and forced Harley's
truck on; it would almost stop, then the lug tires would find
traction and we'd lunge ahead.

"Kind of rough, isn't it?" I said, spinning the wheel to
straighten the sliding truck again.

"I'm used to it," Annie said, looking out her window at
the boiling current little Casey Creek had become. Except
for her mud-spattered boots, Annie was dressed for town.
Maybe because I'd so seldom seen her in a dress, I kept
glancing over. She looked tired, like she was about ready to
cry.

"I thought Amy looked pretty good today."

Annie shook her head, reached into her patent leather
purse, and removed a can of Skoal. She twisted off the tin
lid, dipped a pinch, and put it below her lip. She held out
the can, but I shook my head. "You tell Smoke thanks for
me," Annie said. "He's been right there when I needed him."

"She'll be home in a few days, you'll see."

Mud flew from the churning front wheels and speckled
the windshield. Casey Creek ran across the road ahead, cutting away at the fill above a clogged culvert. I eased the
truck on, unsure of how deep the hole might be. The front
wheels sank, hit solid ground, and pulled us through.

"Road will be out by morning," Annie said. "Some country. It's always all or nothing."

We rounded a brush-lined curve and saw a new-looking
trailer house crosswise up ahead, blocking most of the road.
Several men stood beside the mired tin structure, looking at
its sunken wheels. All the windows on our side had cracked
from the strain of twisting.

I stuffed my pants legs into Harley's rubber milking boots
and climbed out.

"Go on ahead!" a man in striped coveralls yelled. "You
can get around there."

"Where do you think you're going with that?"

"We were supposed to take it up there," he answered, waving at the new road above us on Harris Hill.

"You're a week late. The frost is out of the ground."

"Thanks. I'd never noticed that," he said, and turned away in disgust to help the others shove planks under the trailer's frame.

I drove around the sunken rear of the trailer and on up the road to Amy's turnoff. Annie rode in silence, alternately looking from a sheaf of bills and mail to the raw wet land beyond her window. "Those two weeks of intensive care are going to break me," she said. "That and the legal fees for the lawsuit."

"Doesn't Amy have insurance?"

Annie tucked the packet of papers into her purse. "Do you have insurance?" she asked.

The truck lurched, sank, and stopped. I restarted the engine, put the transfer case in low range, and tried to back out of the sinkhole. The tires spun and the truck settled to its frame in the mud. I tried again, then turned off the key.

"Now we're stuck," I said. I tried to open my door. It was wedged shut, so I climbed through the window and splashed around to Annie's side. She wormed out, and I helped her to the ground. We stood for a minute, looking at the buried wheels and at the water filling our tracks. I put my hands in my pockets and leaned against the hood, feeling the warm wind lift my hair. "Let me know if you change your mind," I said, trying to smile.

"I'm going home." She took off her long coat, folded it over her shoulder, and kissed me on the cheek. "I'll be all right," she said. "Thanks just the same."

I watched her walk off across the prairie, the mud sucking at her boots and spattering her dress. I watched until she was out of sight in the brush along Rocker Gulch, then locked the truck and angled to higher ground as I headed for Harley's. We might have gone along as we had, Annie and I, living on our separate places, riding together and teasing each other. There might have been more, an alliance against the years alone, a closeness born of place. I looked back for her, but by then she was beyond the gulch, crossing the grassy flat below her gate, well past the range of my voice.

I crested the ridge on Cutler Hill and started down toward the Homestead fence, where I could see my roan running with the wind, his tail, high and feathered, sassy behind him, his rough mane lofting as he loped. Clods of muddy duff flew from his hooves, and he pretended to shy as they came down, half bucking, half frisking, imagining, perhaps, a herd of mares and a prairie without wire. I could feel it too in the wind, the promise of spring and more, that lifted the horse, even alone and gelded, to run against himself.

41

I dismantled Summer's weights and boxed the iron plates for storage. Before taping the last carton closed, I added the photograph of Annie that had stood so long on my brother's side of the desk. I worked through the night, cleaning and rearranging the house to suit me, with the exception of Harley's room, which I left closed.

As I carried out the ashes from the kitchen range, streaks of light brightened the eastern sky. The morning was calm, as if, after the Chinook, the world was again at rest. I could hear an airliner in Helena, accelerating off the runway, climbing free of the land. Although it was clear and cold, I stood in my shirt-sleeves and watched the dappled sky until the plane came into sight above the bluffs beyond the barn. As it roared past overhead, I waved.

Lonnie Ford drove into the yard moments after I returned to the house. I took an extra cup from the hooks in the high-backed cabinet and stepped onto the porch.

"Jack," he said, climbing from the battered pickup, "there's been a bad accident."

"Now what," I asked, watching his face as he walked toward me.

Lonnie stopped at the edge of the porch. "It wasn't really an accident, but it happened. I was taking the kids up to meet Schillings just now to catch a ride to school, and I found your horse. He's in the cattle guard."

"In the rails?"

"Yes," Lonnie said, lifting his dark hands as if holding a large trout, "he is. Dogs were running him, and I guess he tried to jump across."

"Come on inside and warm up. I need my jacket."

As I pulled on my herder's coat I was struck by how clear some objects in the kitchen appeared in the early light: the tin salt shaker, the jar of pens and pencils, the dusty can of long neglected hot-chocolate mix, all seemed brand new, or the way I'd seen them a long time ago.

I remembered the roan running the evening before. "How do you know it was dogs?" I asked.

"I shot one. They were still there, tormenting him."

"Any broken bones?"

Lonnie glanced away and nodded. "The way it looks, he almost made it."

I took a box of Krag cartridges from the dish cupboard and lifted the rifle from its hiding place.

"I didn't want to do anything until you knew," he said.

I hesitated, holding the cold rifle barrel in one hand. "Thanks," I told him. "You did the right thing."

"I'll go out for you, if you want."

I opened the box of shells, took four of the 220-grain elk loads and put them in my pocket. "I guess I'll go on out myself."

Lonnie turned at his pickup. "If you need any help, give me a call. I've got that Farmhand."

I headed north across the frozen mud and stubble, wearing my leather boots outside for the first time in months. Patches of ground fog rose from hidden valleys in the Elkhorns; a quarter moon rode the western sky.

By the time I stepped from the timber, the sun had risen above the distant Spokane Hills, lighting the foothills of the Belts in hazy, pink relief. Even the naked prairie before me seemed warm and rich in the golden light. Ahead, I could see the horse, stretched on the rails of the cattle guard, and not far from him, the black, shaggy carcass of a large dog. I walked toward him, feeling my pulse pounding beneath my chin.

Out of habit, I spoke to him as I neared the pole cattle guard. He pointed his ears ahead, then back toward the sound of my voice. Lonnie had left the wire gate open beside the guard. I hung the rifle on the gatepost, and, shielding my eyes from the morning sun, looked down into the pit beneath the rails at the roan's twisted legs. Both the cannon bones in his hind legs had broken midway between the chestnut and fetlock joints. The bones stuck through his skin, jagged and sharp and white.

He'd put up a fight to free himself, cutting the cornet behind the hoof on his right front foot on a rusty sheet of tin nailed to the outside rail. He had severed a big artery, but who could think a horse would have so much blood that it would lie in actual pools on the frozen bottom of the hole? Who would believe that anything could bleed so much and still be alive?

By some miracle of balance or luck, he'd kept his front feet free. I knelt and tried to lift his head. His upper lip quivered, baring his long, yellowed teeth. *Chalmers says he's a four-year-old, but he's six or seven.* He scraped a front hoof on the ground beyond the guard and groaned as I lifted his head onto my knees. *Hellish stout. He will give you something to do while you get back on your feed.*

"You worthless, no-good plug," I told him. "You've really fixed us now." In the dark orb of the eye he turned to me, I saw myself, my bent shoulders and twisted face. Without thinking I tried to lift him standing. I got my shoulder under his neck and chin and lifted, feeling for an instant that I could lift anything, even this whole, half-dead horse. I was surprised to hear myself, as if from the treeline, cursing and crying and struggling to do what could not be done.

He reared himself upright, and I pushed against his shoulder with mine until he came to a three-point stance on his outstretched forelegs, like a dog sitting on his haunches. His lip curled and his eyes rolled with shock. I laid my hand on his neck and felt the quivering muscles beneath his hide. In the pit below the rails I could see his left hind leg twisted half around, the hoof turned east, while the top of him aimed west. He swayed, pointed his chin at the sky, and groaned.

I stood back and felt for a moment I was about to black out. No veterinarian in the world could put his legs back together; I couldn't get him out alive, and neither of us could take any more. The fence and fields wobbled with a dizzy darkness I recognized, and I knew I could go into it forever to hide.

I picked up the rifle and dug the shells from my pocket. I snapped two into the magazine box, closed the bolt on the first one, and stepped back, trying to steady the bead between his eye and ear, where his forelock lay in a long, untrimmed line. My hands shook, my eyes watered, and my trembling legs felt as if I were standing on liquid. I lowered the old rifle and said out loud, "Sweet Jesus, let me do this one thing right." I was talking to the mud and to the sky and to myself, but at the sound of my voice, the roan turned to look at me.

I raised the Krag and fired.

Although he was dead when he struck the rails, he loped a long minute on his side, running like a sun-warmed colt dreaming of racing the windburned land. He galloped, and the quivers of his life ran through him and out of him, and he was gone.

I opened the rifle bolt and removed the empty—*No Brass, No Ammo, Sir!*—and the extra, unexpended round. I hung the rifle back on the gatepost and sat down on the rails, leaning against his spotted rump. I pulled up my legs and laid my head on my folded arms. The sun warmed me through my clothes and dried my face.

Little gray birds worked the tumbleweeds caught in the fence wire, whistling and weaving in their morning flight. Beside the road, the dog lay stretched in the sun, as if it too slept. I wondered how my father and my grandfather had survived so many years alone, but I no longer wondered why.

42

My legs and ass were numb when I lifted my head; the sun had climbed behind me, and it warmed my shoulders. I hobbled on my wooden legs to the rifle, then limped past the dog and down the muddy road toward home. I knew I'd have to pry off the rails and drag him out with the truck. And I knew I should do it soon.

Instead, I turned off the road and walked toward the Veracruz mine. Once, when Harley had worked underground as a boy, there had been a boardinghouse, blacksmith shop, steam boilers, even a garden kept by a Chinese cook. But the silver had been inconsistent, the vein between limerock and granite remained elusive until the miners finally went away.

I stood in the shadow of the heavy-timbered hoist frame and looked at the tailing dump above me, where clusters of pyrite glittered in the midday sun. Since Harley had worked here, four of us had gone to war, wars that had only wounded our sense of peace. And that was why, perhaps, we'd each returned to this place to stay.

As I climbed the dump, I wondered if I could climb the gallus frame too. I shaded my eyes and looked up, to where the squared, inward-sloping timbers joined at a decaying platform, thirty feet or more above the center of the gaping shaft. What had Harley said? . . . *mucking on the number-three level . . . just like when I was a kid, only you were with me . . . the whole end of the tunnel lit up bright as day, like they'd blasted right into the sky.*

I started up, using rust-pitted bolts and block braces for footholds, climbing hand over hand up the rotten timbers toward the open-centered platform where the blocks and sheaves once hung. The great wooden uprights had rotted to their cores, and the gallus frame moved as I climbed. *Down two hundred feet, working in carbide light, mud to your knees.* Slowly I pulled myself onto the platform, squared myself on a morticed cross-timber, and let my legs dangle over the inside edge. From where I sat, I could see the entire length of the snowbound Elkhorn Range and the foothills below, bared already by the recent Chinook winds. South of me, beyond the creek, the hay fields lay in gold relief among the monuments of granite and random clusters of trees. I swung my legs and looked down, and thought how easy it would be to close my eyes, lean forward just a little, and disappear. I wondered if that's how Harley's father had felt, confronted finally by these same senseless hills, this same empty sky.

I could see the top twenty feet of the hole, the drill grooves still visible in the powder-shattered rock. *You were with me, and we were shoveling mud, when one of the drillers hollers back, "Fire in the hole!"*

I tipped back my head, looking from the definite black below to the infinite blue above. Garrett's favorite expression: Fire in the hole. A phrase he'd used for topics from war to sex. Garrett in the hole now forever. Garrett at the gates of Hillbilly Heaven. . . . And I remembered clearly leaning over that fuse, telling the boy they sometimes turned hard, forcing the spanner while thinking about where you were, twisting and not paying any mind to how the mechanism turned all at once, just hurrying to get another round in the air.

For an instant, clouds scudding above me made it seem the gallus frame was moving instead, as if my weight had sprung a delicate balance between geometrical strength and decay, and that the entire structure was twisting, collapsing into the hole. I kicked out my feet trying to save myself, and a rotten plank broke loose, tumbling and twisting into the darkness. It did not fall far before I heard it land, and when I looked down into the pit, toward the lapping sound of impact, I knew I would not fall. *And we were shoveling mud. Cold, muddy, dripping son of a bitch.*

I held one of the live cartridges between the tips of my fingers and let it go. *Shoveling mud in the damned dark.* I dropped another round and another, hearing each time a hollow percolating pock as they hit.

I looked across the flat, from the roan, bloody now and shrunken by death, to the lone pine at the end of the hidden lane, and I remembered sparks of time before my memory began: dripping stone walls in tunnels where hooded oilskins were worn against the trickling wet; dust pulled by thirty head of horses pushed at a hard run toward the hidden corral; the rising airborne ecstasy of that one clean ride.

I leaned out over the darkness, stretched my arm, and dropped the last, the empty cartridge into the hole my grandfather had helped to dig. And I heard again the enduring, echoing sound of water.